THE ADVENTURES OF SHIREEN GREENE
AND THE BEACON OF LIFE

BY ANTHONY PAUKOVITS

Copyright © 2020 Anthony Paukovits

MR ANTHONY PAUKOVITS

Dedication

This book is dedicated to the memory of my
Father and Cousin who always encouraged me to
be the best that I can be, in everything I do.

Acknowledgement

I would like to thank my pal Matt for all of his continued support, encouragement and artictic talent which has helped to make this book a reality.

PROLOGUE

SHIREEN GREENE AND THE BEACON OF LIFE, IS THE FIRST OF MANY ENCHANTED STORIES OF A GIRL THAT DEVELOPS INTO A YOUNG WOMAN, EMBARKING ON INTREPID JOURNEYS INTO THE UNKNOWN, ENCOUTERING EVILS BOTH KNOWN AND NOT KNOWN TO THE REALM OF LIFE.

MAKING NEW ACQUAINTANCES, FRIENDS AND ENTITIES, AS SHE TRAVELS THE UNLIMITED REALMS AND WORLDS OF GOOD AND EVIL.

STANDING FIVE SIX INCHES TALL, HAS THE PERSONALITY OF SOMEONE WHO CAN BE A KIND, UNDERSTANDING, FIERY ADVERARY, A LETHAL COMBINATION, SHE IS RECRUITED BY THE ORDER OF THE LIFE TO JOIN THE CIRCLE OF LIFE, THAT GIVES LIFE, SHE HAS BEEN CHOSEN TO BECOME A PROTECTOR.

A PROTECTOR IS A PERSON OR ENTITY WHO HAS BEEN SPECIALLY CHOSEN, TO BECOME OR ALREADY IS, A PROTECTOR OF THE   BEACON AND ORDER OF LIFE.

TRUTH, JUSTICE & HONESTY, SIMILAR TO THE JAPANESE BUSHIDO WARRIOR CODE, KNIGHTS OF THE ROUND TABLE HAD THEIR OWN CODE. AND SO DO THE PROTECTORS HAVE THEIR OWN CODE OF ETHICS, THAT BELONG TO THE CIRCLE OF LIFE, PROTECTORS THAT SERVE THE ORDER OF LIFE, ALL GAVE AN OATH OF TRUTH, JUSTICE & HONESTY.

ALL SERVE THE BEACON OF LIFE, WHICH GIVES LIFE.

CHAPTER ONE
THE CHURCH FETE.

In the principality of Wales, where Welsh royalty once ruled this fine nation. where dragons, magicians and druids once lived. Where wizards, warlocks and witches practised their black arts, battles for the principality of Wales took place, the Saxons, the English and the Normans over hundreds even thousands of years, tried to subdue the Welsh nation.

Owain Glyndwr, Gwenllian, Owain ap Dafydd, Llywelyn the great, Branwen ferch Llyr, Princess Nest, just a few of the heroes and heroines of Wales.

Did they fade into time or did they escape to another dimension or realm, was it that they just visited Wales then escape back to their dimension or realm, the truth will never be known, or will it!

In the small Welsh coastal town of Nusea, lives a 15-year-old girl by the name of Shireen Greene, like all 15-year olds, Shireen enjoys life with her friends, goes to school willingly sometimes and not so willingly other times, your typical teenager, saying that she is a good student on the whole, when she wants to be, the family home is a modest three-bedroom house a little conservatory at the rear of the house, A cabin at the bottom of the garden, better known as dad's man cave.

Shireen's family consists of her dad, Jason Greene, mum, Emma Greene and her pain in the ass brothers Harry Greene aged 10 and George Greene aged 8, as you can imagine there is no love lost sometimes between siblings, for the odd push and shove and some abusive words are not uncommon, in the Greene household

Well, its Friday afternoon, its teatime everybody is home, Shireen is in the kitchen giving mum a hand to prepare tea, brothers Harry and George are being their usual pain in the backsides asking when the tea is going to be ready. Dad is just washing his hands after fixing the boys bikes, dad's mobile rang out, dad answers his phone, "Hello Jake "Jake is dad's brother .

Dad and uncle Jake are like a couple of schoolboys, always giggling and chuckling, I would go as far to say, a pair of giggling schoolgirls taking a shine to some boy they had just met.

After dad's phone call he announces," We are going to a church fete tomorrow". Just to put you the picture dad and my uncle think they are a pair of shrewd antique collectors, well, some of the time, they do get lucky.

Shireen normally tries to escape out of outings like this saying, "I'm meeting my friends", the only thing is Shireen's friends have their compulsory family things to do this weekend, which they all enjoy, NOT. So, Shireen thinks to herself, well it is time out of the house, better than being on my own, I might get something out of this little trip.

As Shireen and her family sit down for their tea, which consisted of curly cheesy fries, burgers, salad and chicken strips, just to shut her siblings up, Shireen's brothers are constantly nagging, how long tea was going to be, it is easier for her mum to make a quick something to eat, as she had been working all day at the local doctors as a receptionist.

Shireen thought to herself, how it would be if she had been an only child, then looked at her brothers with an absolute look of disdain and horror, though they do come in handy when I need someone to blame.

As tea had just finished, Uncle Jake phoned again, Jason Greene answered the phone "Hi their bro, what can I do for you?"

Jason Greene wandered off talking to his brother, Shireen's delightful pain in the ass brothers, decided to play some computer games, Shireen and her mum did the clearing away as usual.

Mum turned to Shireen and said jokingly "I swear your father has your uncle to phone him, just to get out of doing the washing up" then Emma Green chuckled and Shireen gave a little laugh as well.

Shireen turned to her mum, with a little look of evilness and the thoughts were just as bad and said: "Why don't you let the boys do the washing up".

Emma Greene turned to Shireen, then burst out laughing, then said "Can you imagine your brothers doing the washing up, I would like to have some plates and mugs left in the house "talking of mugs Shireen thought to herself, how can I sort out those pair of mugs out, mean her delightful siblings, as her brothers went skulking towards the biscuit box on top of the fridge, without even looking, Shireen's mum said " No you don't, early bed for everyone, we all have to be up early"

Harry and George stood there, what can only be described as faces like a smacked ass, Shireen just laughed, Harry turned to his mum and said, "I wasn't doing anything" Emma Greene turned to Harry and said, "You know what happened to Pinocchio for telling lies" Emma Greene proceeded to say" Star Wars has the force, I have mothers have intuition "then turned to Shireen winked and they both laughed very loudly.

Harry and George thought it was in their best interest to make a hasty retreat to their computer games.

With that Jason Greene made an appearance, Emma Green turned and said, "Nice of you to make an appearance" Jason Greene replied that was my brother, the reply was" that's a surprise" and laughed.

Jason Greene replied, "you never guess what, we are going to a church fete tomorrow, possibly a lot of cheap goodies to be had" Jason Greene further went onto say" Oh, ah, my brother

Marcus is coming with us tomorrow, he is home from his business trip".

Jason Greene added "We are meeting at Kev's cafe', looks like my brother is treating us all to a cooked breakfast",

Jason Greene liked his brother, knowing what he had been through during his life with his wife's illness, Marcus Greene always remained positive, always available when needed by his brothers, Jason Greene had total respect for his brother Marcus.

Judging by the look on Jason Greene's face, he knew that he was going to have not as much fun as he thought.

Shireen and Emma Greene gave a little dance, a little wiggle, rather loud yes with laughter straight afterwards, Jason Greene replied to their happiness by saying "I thought might make both of you happy", Shireen replied "It sure does dear father" then gave a somewhat bemused chuckle.

Emma Greene then turned to Jason Greene smirking and said, "Well that's you and your brother knackered, are going to be good boys' tomorrow, you know Marcus will put the both of you in your places without saying anything if you are bad boys" Emma Greene went on to say, "This is going to be absolute joy tomorrow".

Just an insight to Marcus Greene, the eldest of three siblings, Marcus Greene a man of little words, the looks that he can convey, will either be of disdain or happiness, a blank expression is just to confuse the hell out of you.

Nevertheless, Marcus Greene was a kind and generous man, especially towards his nieces and nephews, Shireen Greene loved and respected her uncle Marcus, they often engaged in deep conversation about the universe and other topics that Shireen had in common with her uncle.

Marcus Greene lived alone, his wife Rachel died of cancer four years ago, he loved his wife very much, having no children of his own, he adores his nieces and nephews, he owns a small emporium shop that sold all sorts of objects and jewellery, a successful business, Shireen and her friends often visited her uncle, just to be amazed at the kinds of wonderful objects in the shop.

He often went on buying trips, to some very obscure and far distant lands, leaving his assistant by the name of Andrea to run the shop.Marcus Greene often arrived back from his business trips, with some historical, beautiful, exotic items, when Marcus Greene is away on his business trips, Andrea his one and only employee, looks after the shop when Marcus Greene is away on his trips.

Mum reckons that there is some serious loving going on behind closed doors, sometimes behind shop doors, who really knows, mum always tries her best to press Marcus Greene into confessing, He always reminds Emma Greene that her talents are wasted, and she should have been a police detective.

Emma Greene can only hope for a confession one day, which is not forthcoming now.

Well, it's 8 am, the alarms are going off, there's a mad scramble for the bathroom, Emma Greene wins first prize, Shireen wins a close second prize, Jason Greene is turfing Harry and George out of bed, last night was zombie story night, flashing torches at each other, scary stories, now they are tired and grumpy as hell, Jason Greene informs the two brothers " If you don't get out of bed, I will help you out", a play fight ensues, which results in, Harry being sat on, George in a headlock, with submissions of surrender being protested very strongly.

Shireen was watching the whole incident , Shireen thought "One for Facebook", then proceeded to aim her phone at the groaning entanglement, smirked and said, "Smile, you're going to be famous".

There were protests from all caught in the entanglement, which Shireen replied "Tough",

Shireen went onto say "All of you are going to be famous, expect to be signing autographs". Then she walked away chuckling to herself. Leaving her dad and her siblings to contemplate their newfound fame.

Mum is out the shower, Shireen is just about to enter the bathroom, Harry tries to waltz pass her, which results in a flick of Harry's ear, Harry replies with "That hurt" Shireen replies with " Oh dear" then proceeds to close the door on Harry's foot, which causes Harry to dance around on one foot, Dad and George stood there laughing, pointing fingers and having repeated bursts of laughter.

Finally, everyone is sat around the table for breakfast, bowl cornflakes was had by everyone as a cooked breakfast was too be had by all later that morning, looking at her brother's with contempt Shireen announces, "It's like feeding time at the zoo, I'm looking at a pair of potbelly pigs ", brothers Harry and George reply with grunting noises, which results in a scolding from mum and dad, Shireen smirks with delight and feels justice was swift and true.

Jason Greene's mode of transport is a seven-seat minibus, which doubles as his work vehicle, being a gardener and arborist it came in very handy on most occasions, the minibus has a tow hitch the back, so he can tow his shredding machine, the other thing is that there is plenty of legroom, which cuts down the pushing, shoving and tears. Emma Greene's car is a little run around hatch-back, Life would be extremely uncomfortable for all concerned, if they all had travelled in mum's car there would have been heaps of discontent and trouble.

Which is not good, when it is a family outing, normally ends in tears, mainly for the two boys, as the giggling, pinching, kicking and the wet finger in the ear, results in a look of stop that from mum and a threat of being grounded from dad, so that is why we travel in the minibus.

After usual who decides, who is going sit where the result is the brothers end up sitting on the flip sets, Shireen has the more comfortable back seat, putting on her headphones, to cut out the insane conversations that Harry and George participate in, Mum and dad sat in the front, which gave them a certain amount of noise reduction, which was a blessing to them. After about ten minutes into the journey Jason Greene's phone rings, the ringtone is load crap, a god-awful remix of some shit tune that Jason Greene thinks is awesome, Emma Greene looks at Jason Greene and said to Jason Greene "What the hell is that" Jason Greene replies, "That's good music" the reply came straight back " Maybe for tone-deaf people", then proceeded to mock and laugh at Jason Greene.

By the time they discussed the merits of the song the caller had rung off, Emma Greene looks at the phone and says "Well, well, that's a surprise, it's your brother" and Emma Greene laughed, then says "There's a message, this should be interesting, let us see what intellectual words of wisdom your brother has for us today".

With that the message was left on the answer phone played on the hands-free speaker, "Hello, bro give us a ring ", Emma Greene laughed and said "Your bother should have been a man of literature" Jason Greene replied in a not too happy voice" you are always having to go about my bro" a reply comes back fast and furious "Well, it's not just me, Jakes wife Sally has said you two can be a right pair of ding-a-lings when you want to be "and proceeded to laugh, Jason Greene knew that second prize was imminent if he carried on, so decided to say nothing instead" Give my bro a ring for me, pretty please" shaking his head as he knew he had been beaten in the verbal exchange.

So, Emma Greene rang Jake Greene's phone, then a then reply was "Hello" the reply back from Emma Greene was "This is the institute for the tone-deaf, I believe you left us a message", Emma Greene could not help but laugh, there was a burst of laughed from Sally Greene on the phone, Sally Greene said " Hi Emma " the reply came back "Hi Sally " Sally said " Don't tell they have got the same shit ringtone" Emma went onto say " How is your half of the ding-a- ling brothers looking, has he got a face like a smacked ass" Sally replied "

Most definitely" they both laughed Sally then said, "Send me a pic of your half of the ding-a- ling brothers, I will send you a pic of mine".

With that Emma Greene said to Jason Greene" smile", Emma and Sally are more like sisters, rather than a sister-in-law, after all the banter had stopped, Sally Greene went on to say that Marcus Greene had invited everyone to breakfast at Kevin's café," a nice clean café, where the food was good and reasonable.

As the Greene's arrived Marcus Greene was standing outside Kevin's café, A man about five foot, eight inches tall, broad shoulders, smartly dressed in a light blue shirt, sports jacket and dark pair of chino trousers, with a dark tan, exceptionally clean pair of shoes, also waiting was Jake Greene with his wife Emma, daughter Abbey and son Tom.

Marcus Greene had already been to see the owner Kevin and organised tables, which was not a problem as the early morning rush had finished, Kevin the owner was glad for any extra trade this time of the morning, this was his quiet period.

Everybody said their hello's, hugs and kisses, Marcus Greene announced that they should go inside, Sally Greene turned to Emma Greene and said "Have you seen those two" meaning Jason and Jake Greene,

"They are on their best behaviour" Sally grinned like a Cheshire cat and winked at Emma Greene; Emma Greene replied "It's going to be a long and remarkably interesting day" they both laughed. Marcus, Jake and Jason Greene walked together, talking about football and other sports, the boy's Harry, George and Tom walked together, discussing how to survive a zombie apocalypse, Shireen and Abbey talked about school, exams, then talked about most important things, boys, music and makeup.

Everyone found where and whom they wanted to sit by; Shireen Greene found herself with Abbey on her left, Uncle Marcus on her right, Kevin the owner came and took everyone's orders, proceeded back to the kitchen, a waitress brought over teas and coffees, orange juices for Shireen and cousins.

Marcus Greene said, "This is a no better time than any other" What everyone failed to notice, that in the confusion of everyone deciding who was going to sit where Marcus Greene had slipped back out to his car to retrieve a tanned holdall, everyone was in anticipation of what gifts they are about to receive.

Marcus Greene turned to his nephews and retrieved three watches of showing the crests of their favourite football teams, Marcus Greene then turned to his brothers and said," You pair of wasters have you been good boys" everyone laughed including Jason and Jake Greene, Marcus Greene turned to Emma and Sally Greene and reiterated the question "Have they been good boys "in acknowledgement they replied in unison " Well I suppose they have been good boys" then laughed.

Marcus Greene produced two bottles of very expensive brandy, said to his brothers "I hope you enjoy" said Marcus Greene, "Thanks bro" replied Jason and Jake Greene Then turned to Emma and Sally Greene said "As for you my most gorgeous looking and delight full ladies", Marcus Greene dived back into the holdall and retrieved two boxes, Marcus gave one box to Emma Greene and a box Sally Greene, you could see the absolute delight in their faces, cautiously they both opened the boxes, they then retrieved a gold bangle each with all sorts of glittering items on the bangle from each , both stood up, proceeded to give Marcus Greene a hug and a kiss on the cheek, then sat back down admiring their newly acquired gift,

Marcus Greene turned and said "Now for my two favourite princesses", Marcus Greene pulled out two boxes from his holdall and said "I hope you like these gifts young ladies, "Marcus Greene stood up, opened one box, Shireen and Abbey looked at each other with delight and anticipation, then Marcus Greene produced a pendant from one of the boxes, the pendant, was of sliver chain and a hexagon-shaped item hanging on the chain, there was a handcrafted engraving of some sort of ancient animal on it.

Marcus Greene placed the pendant around Shireen's neck, Marcus Greene opened the other box, then produced another pendant, the same again white silver chain, this chain had all sorts of items around the chain, in the centre was a face of a woman on a round silver disc, then placed it around Abbey's neck.

Just as everyone said thank you again and Marcus Greene was about to sit down, he said "I nearly forgot, I missed Shireen's birthday while I was away on my travels, Marcus Greene sat down, he then produced the last of the items from his holdall, it was a sea-green box, Marcus Greene turned to Shireen, then said " A belated happy birthday" Shireen was absolutely beaming, she had thought her favourite uncle had forgotten about her birthday, Shireen was ecstatic about her extra gift and that her uncle had remembered her birthday, everyone clapped, even the one or two who remained in the café also joined in and clapped, Shireen was so happy she had to give her uncle a hug and a kiss on the cheek.

Everyone urged Shireen to open the box, Shireen opened the box slowly, everyone looked on in excitement, the lid of the box came off to reveal a silver coin with a gold edge, with a double dragon's head in the centre of it, on the flip side what you could only describe as an odd-looking beacon, Marcus leant over towards Shireen and said "This is a very special coin", Shireen looked at the coin with marvel, with that Kevin and one of the waitresses started bringing the breakfasts out. Everyone started talking amongst themselves, what they had done, what they had been up to.

Emma Greene turned to Marcus Greene and said, "Where did you go" Marcus Greene replied "Well, would you believe me if told you "and just laughed Marcus Greene then replied, "I have been around Persia and the middle east, looking for new stock for my emporium".

Emma and Sally Greene couldn't resist the temptation of asking, "Well Marcus, how is the lovely Andrea", asked a sheepish Sally Greene, then both of his brothers decided to add their interest to the conversation, Jason Greene said with a smirk and a nudge from his brother Jake, "Yes, dear brother how is the very delightful Andrea "Marcus Greene looked his brothers with a smirk and a pondering look on his face and said "Andrea, well she is good thanks for asking "he also replied, "In fact, really good as those bumps I left on your heads, when the both of you tried to fight me as kids, what a pair of beautiful bumps I left you with".

Everyone fell about laughing; Emma Greene turned to Sally Greene and said "What did I say, entertaining for us, not so entertaining for those pair of ding a lings", they both could not control their laughter, neither could the children

Jason and Jake tried to laugh off the comments, they knew not to carry it on, as it could result in more ridicule and laughter from their spouses and offspring.

Emma Greene persisted in her questioning of Marcus Greene "Is there going to a booty call tonight, Marcus?".

Marcus Greene with a smouldering grin leant across the table and said "Yes", Emma and Sally Greene sat up and leant forward like a pair of hounds that had caught the scent of a fox, together Emma and Sally Greene said with a cunning simile, thinking that Marcus Greene had finally cracked "Please, do go on "Marcus Greene leant over the table with a sincere look and whispered "I'm going to a have rendezvous at eight tonight" By this time, everyone was on the edge of their seats.

Sally Greene then took over the questioning, "Marcus, please feel free to carry on", by this time Shireen Greene thought, knowing her uncle he was going to play a blinder, and he did.

Marcus Greene softly took Sally Greene's hand, placed both his hands around Sally's hand and gazed straight into eyes and said softly "I'm having a rendezvous with a six-pack, a bottle of malt whiskey and a takeaway". Everyone around, including Kevin the owner of the café burst out laughing.

Sally Greene leant forward and said, "Your absolute rotter" ,laughed and said, "I still adore you", Emma Greene nodded in agreeance.

Emma Greene then interrupted and said "Anything exciting to come? Marcus Greene replied "Plenty", Sally Greene then chimed in and said "Like what? "

Marcus Greene replied, "That my dear princess, you will have to wait and see when everything arrives at my emporium " Sally Greene interrupts with "Marcus Greene you're such a smooth talker" laughed and further said " I'm sure I married the wrong brother" and laughed, at that point Emma Greene butted and said "Me too" they both giggled like a pair of blushing schoolgirls.

To save any more embarrassing comments for Emma and Sally Greene, Kevin the owner of the café approached Marcus Greene and said "Is everything ok? Everyone agreed, which pleased the café owner.

Marcus Greene turned to Shireen and said "That is very special coin , in time, maybe sooner than you think, the coin will reveal how special and importance of the coin ", Shireen looked at her uncle with a look of confusion and wonder, she was still happy with her gifts and before she could enquire what her uncle had meant, Abbey interrupted Shireen's thinking on what her uncle meant, asked if she could have a look at the coin, by then Shireen had lost her thoughts on the subject, both girls proceeded into a deep conversation about all things trivial.

Marcus Greene could see time was getting on and decided to take charge, in a firm but pleasing manner said "Right, ladies and gentlemen we need to make our way to the church hall", everyone thanked Marcus Greene for their breakfast, then proceeded to remark how lovely the breakfast was to Marcus Greene and Kevin the café owner, Kevin replied to everyone by saying" I'm happy that you all enjoyed, please call again", Marcus Greene paid the bill and gave a generous tip, then followed everyone out of the café.

Marcus Greene turned to everyone and said "See you all at the church hall", everybody replied "Yes, see you there Marcus" Shireen then butted in and said to her mum "Mum, can I go with uncle Marcus in his car" Shireen's mum replied "I'm ok with it, have you asked your uncle ?", Marcus Greene just laughed, then shook his head in amusement, then said "I just don't know if I should", Shireen then gave it the old puppy eyes look, then said to her uncle in a pouting I'm a sad little girl way "Please, uncle Marcus can I travel in your car to the church fete", Shireen already knew the answer, even before she had asked the question, Marcus Greene replied "You know very well that you can", shook his head again in amusement and grinned.

Marcus and Shireen got into a sea-green estate car, Shireen's parents and brothers got into dad's minibus, Jake Greene and family got into their red estate car, as Shireen travelled with her uncle, she remembered the question she wanted to ask him "Uncle Marcus, can I ask you what you meant about the coin, back at the café?".

Marcus looked at Shireen and replied "Patience is a virtue, my dear, time will reveal all "Shireen did not want to make an issue about the coin, so she decided to talk about her uncles' trip to Persia and the middle east.

As Marcus and Shireen arrived at the church fete, Marcus Greene stopped his car and said "Shireen, please bring that coin I gave you, I would like to test some of these so-called antique dealers.

Shireen, turned her towards her uncle, then gave an evil smirk and replied "Are we going to have some fun today Uncle Marcus?"Marcus Greene gave a little chuckle and had that same evil smirk that Shireen had on her face, replied "We surely are my dear Shireen, we surely are", As everyone went off into their little groups, Emma and Sally Greene decided they needed a coffee, went and sat down at the improvised café, the boys went to try their luck on some of the games that were on offer, Jason and Jake Greene, wheelers and dealers extraordinaire, went off to try and make their millions.

Shireen Greene was still sporting her somewhat, innocent, but evil grin, she wanted to see her uncle do his thing, especially against those unethical robbing leeches, As Marcus Greene would describe them.

There was a tap on Marcus Greene's shoulder, Marcus Greene turned around and saw it was Abbey Greene, Abbey said, "Can I tag along with you two?", Marcus Greene replied, "Of course my dear Abbey".

As the three of them proceed along with the many stalls, Shireen informed Abbey of the impending fun that was in store for them, Shireen and Abbey nudged each other and smiled, as they got to the back of the church hall, the three of came to what Marcus Greene describes as thieves' corner.

Marcus Greene turned to his nieces and said, "Ladies the fun is about to begin", Marcus Greene turned to Abbey and said, "I believe Shireen has informed you of our little escapade, now ladies I will lead, you play along".

The two girls gave a little laugh and nodded their heads, Marcus Greene then said "Let the fun begin", Marcus Greene and his two co-conspirators browsed the last remaining couple stalls, when there was a voice "Can I help you "Marcus Greene replied in a blunt and straight to the point voice" No me and my daughters are just browsing," as the man was about to turn away, Marcus Greene gave a little forced to cough and said "Actually, there may be something you can help me with", the man who was dressed as some chancer, turned back around very quickly and replied, "What might that be?".

Marcus Greene proceeded to say "My daughter has a coin that was left to her in a will, by a great aunt, would you be so kind and take a look at it", The chancer, spun like a dancer and replied, "Yes, I would be glad to take a look", Marcus Greene turned to Shireen, smiled and winked then "Could I have the coin please", Shireen pulled a box from her jacket pocket and replied with a smirk "Here is the box father "and again smirked.

As Marcus Greene opened up the box, the man's eyes lit up like a pair of headlights on a car, on full beam, the man soon realised that his cheesy smile could give the game away, the chancer cleared his throat and said",

"It's a lovely old coin, not worth a lot, maybe thirty pounds", Marcus Greene had to turn away nearly choked with laughter trying not to give the game away, both Abbey and Shireen placed their hand over their mouths, to hide their smirking, after Marcus Greene composed himself, he turned and said in a emphasized trying to sound amazing voice "That much, NEVER", by this time a flock of chancers had descended around the coin, trying to buy the coin, there was a bit of a squabble going on, who had seen the coin first.

Marcus Greene trying to keep his composer turned and said "If you can't play nicely, I'm taking the coin back", Marcus Greene took the coin and box back of the chancer, put the coin back in the box, gave the box and coin back to Shireen, put one arm around each of his nieces and said laughingly "That's how you stir the shit ladies", then proceeded to walk down the other side of the church hall, both Shireen and Abbey fell about laughing.

As all three walked back down the other side of the church hall, in the corner of the church hall, Marcus Greene, spotted an attractive middle-aged woman, about five foot four inches tall, long brown, medium build, selling all sorts of trinkets, Marcus Greene said to Shireen and Abbey, "Let us go and investigate", both girls agreed to the suggestion, as Marcus Greene with nieces in tow approached the table, the woman "Hi there anything you are looking for?", Marcus Greene replied in a rather smitten voice "We are just looking thanks, do you mind my nieces peruse your items "the lady replied "My name is Sandra, yes they can peruse as much as they want" then they both laughed.

Shireen looked at Abbey, Abbey looked at Shireen, they both gave a wink and a cheeky grin, Shireen said to Abbey "Looks like our uncle has pulled", Abbey pulled her phone out, Shireen asked "You are going to do what I think you are going to do?", Abbey replied "Yep I sure am, this is important information", they both laughed, Abbey then took a sneaky picture of uncle Marcus and his new friend Sandra.

Abbey decides to go and seek out her mum and aunty, Shireen stays with her uncle, Sandra the lady who has got the last table in the fete, Abbey calls her uncle Marcuse's friend the new squeeze, reaches under the table and produces a box then calls Shireen, Sandra then hands the box to Shireen, Shireen looks at the box with some apprehension, Sandra encouraged Shireen to open the box, so did her uncle.

Shireen opens the box cautiously and as she finally reveals the contents of the box, her eyes sparkle like diamonds, she could not believe what she was looking at.

The box revealed a pair of bracelets, the colour of the bracelets changed into a multitude of different colours every time they hit the sunlight, on top of the bracelets lying flat, was what appeared to be a beacon with a sphere on top, the same colour changing phenomenon appears to happen with the beacon and sphere when they also encounter sunlight. The bracelets were not silver, yet were not white; they appeared to be a glowing metallic ivory colour.

Sandra then said to Shireen "Do you like them?" Shireen replied with an extending smile that equalled the brilliance", Shireen then said "Out of curiosity how much are these bracelets, there is no way I could afford them, I would like to know ", Sandra winked at Marcus Greene without Shireen noticing, then gave a little smile and said "Maybe you have something to trade ?", Shireen did not know what to do, the only thing of possible value she had, was the coin her lovely her uncle Marcus had given her for her birthday.

Marcus Greene could see the look of dilemma and confusion on Shireen's face, he then turned her towards him and said with a sympathetic smile" I won't be offended in any way, if you want to trade the coin for the bracelets, just to be clear, I'm encouraging you to do it, it's a good trade", Shireen produced the coin from her jacket pocket and said to Sandra " Will this do" Sandra took the box from Shireen, opened it, Sandra then looked at Shireen then said, "This is a lovely coin, where did you get it?" Shireen went onto say that it was a present from her uncle.

Sandra not wanted to show to eager, pulled a few faces made a few "Maybes'", then finally said the words Shireen was hoping for "Ok, it's a deal ", Shireen was ecstatic about the trade, she then had a feeling that their paths again," then a voice that seems to be in her head, the voice of her uncle that said" Your paths will cross again", it gave her the shivers, she looked around, her uncle was just standing there smiling, she thought to herself that's weird.

Just as the deal was done, who should be making an entrance, it was Shireen's cousin Abbey guiding Emma and Sally Greene, making a direct line towards Marcus Greene, especially after the information Abbey had passed on, then the unforgettable tones of Emma Greene's voice said "Well, well, Marcus Greene, you sly old dog, who's your new friend "then Sally Greene chimed in with her comment "Yes, Marcus Greene fancy using the pretence of church fete to go on the pull", Marcus Greene, looked at Emma and Sally Greene, with Sandra looking on, wearing a smirk on her face with amusement, said ", My dear princesses, I can see how happy you are married to my brothers, I felt jealous, even envious, that's why I came to see my old friend Sandra "Sally Greene replied " I don't know about the happily married bit" then they all laughed, Emma Greene said "Old friends, special friends maybe?".

With that Sandra, grabbed Marcus Greene's arm, kissed him on the cheek and said," Coffee soon Marcus and don't forget", then left everyone to serve a couple of browsers, while Marcus, Emma and Sally Greene carried on with their banter, Shireen Greene could not help herself and had another look at the bracelets again, with that Abbey Green came towards Shireen, Shireen closed the box and placed the box back in her jacket pocket, for safety she zipped pocket up.

Marcus Greene called Abbey and Shireen over to where everyone else was standing, then announced, "I don't know about anybody else but I'm feeling hungry, its one pm time for lunch" everyone agreed, Emma Greene grabbed one of Marcus Greene's arms, Sally Greene grabbed the other arm, with Abbey and Shireen in tow.

On their way to the car park, Sally Greene said, "Well Marcus", Marcus Greene knew what was coming and just grinned, then said, "What my dear", in quick response Sally Greene said, "Tell us more about sexy Sandra?", Marcus Greene protested his innocence that nothing was going on, he went onto say Sandra was just a friend.

As they got back to their cars Marcus Greene said to his brothers," Any luck?" both answered "Yeah, not bad bro", they all decided to meet at a little pub about a mile down the road, Jason and Jake Greene loaded up their vehicles with their goodies.

Marcus Greene now had Abbey as well as Shireen in his car, so off they went to the Blue Angel for their lunch.

CHAPTER TWO
THE RUMBLINGS

Shireen Greene sat in the front passenger's seat, her cousin Abbey Greene sat in the rear passenger seat directly behind Marcus Greene, there was a lot of back and forth idle chit

chat between the two girls, Shireen looked now and again at her uncle with a perplexed look, Marcus Greene would catch Shireen looking at him, it seemed that he could read her mind, Then just smile at Shireen, Abbey Greene would just blurt on and on, unaware to what was going on, now and again she wasn't sure if she was imagining a vibration in her pocket coming from the box, followed by a warmth transmitting from the box, everyone arrived at the Blue Angel pub, parked their cars, Marcus Greene took the lead with his brothers, Jason and Jake they disappeared into the pub, to organise the tables and have a sneaky pint while doing so, Harry, George and Tom played zombie annihilation in the pub playground, Emma, Sally, Shireen and Abbey sat around a pub table in the beer garden.

Abbey Greene had already informed Emma and Sally Greene that Shireen had swapped the coin that her uncle Marcus had given her as a present, Emma Greene turned to Shireen and said "Let me see it" Shireen replied, "See what, "Emma Greene replied with a dumbfounded look on her face, "The bracelets, you silly girl," Shireen gave a cheeky smile and a sparkle in her eyes and said" Oh that".

Shireen produced the box from her pocket, she started to open the box, it was like a multitude of sunbeams trying to escape the box, in a rush of blinding light, the brightness blinding their eyes, they all admired the brilliance of the bracelets, Sally and Emma Greene could not utter any words, totally speechless.

At that point Marcus Greene appeared from the pub and announced their table was ready, Sally Greene called the three boys, just in time as a little disagreeing was just about to take place, peace had prevailed just in time, as everyone sat around the table Marcus Greene said, " Right ladies and young gentlemen it is just you to order".

There was an awkward glance between Marcus Greene and Shireen as they sat down, Marcus Greene knew that Shireen needed and required more answers than he was prepared at that moment in time, that little voice came back to drive Shireen with desire for knowledge of what about to happen, in the present and the future, in the voice of uncle, kept saying "The future will reveal itself, a little bit at a time".

Shireen looked at her uncle as if the conversation were between their two minds "I understand what you are saying, but why". Before Shireen could finish her sentence, there was a quick flash of a courtyard the size of a football field, she found to be standing next to some sort of massive beacon, the beacon resembled the emblems on her bracelets, the beacons seemed to go on forever with a free-floating sphere on the top, the beacon and sphere could only be described as an ivory white colour, on times the beacon and sphere seemed to pulsate with extreme brightness with twinges of the rainbow flowing from top to bottom.

As Shireen was about to pivot around, there was a sensation of her arm being forcefully pushed by Emma Greene, then asked: "Shireen, what are you going to have?" Shireen replied, " Gammon and chips, please mum," then Marcus Greene's voice in her mind said, " That's a taste of things to come", she tried desperately to answer, the only problem, it was like her mobile had run out of talk time again, Shireen felt as if she was watching a soap tv programme and the titles and the theme music had started leaving her in another cliff hanger episode situation.

Shireen tried to make desperate eye contact with her uncle, unfortunately for her, this was to be a futile exercise on her part, she could see that her uncle was in deep conversation with his brothers, Abbey Greene then interrupted her thoughts asking her advice on a pair of shoes that Abbey had spotted on an online shop, the conversation around the table seemed to be dying a death, at that point, Sally Greene piped up and said "Time to make a move and do some food shopping, hungry mouths to feed", then came a reply from Emma Greene with a slight chuckle in her voice " If it's anything like our house, it must resemble feeding time at the zoo", there was a look of disdain from Jake and Jason Greene followed by a smirk.

Marcus Greene did his usual stealth act left the table to settle the bill, ensuring everything was in the order returned to the table and said "I hope you all enjoyed today, I know I certainly did, the time has beaten us again time to go", there was a general agreeance of nods and smiles on how they all enjoyed, what was perceived early in the day of it's going to be a boring day, held a lot of surprises especially for Shireen Greene.

Everyone left their seats and proceeded outside to the car park, the usual kisses and hugs took place, both Greene families said goodbyes leaving Marcus Greene with a tearful smile, especially missing his deceased wife, turning to his right wiping the corner of his eyes trying not to show his emotions, Shireen and Emma Greene stood right in front of Marcus Greene, guessing the emotions of what Marcus Greene must be feeling, the slight watery eyes did give the game away, Emma and Shireen gave Marcus Greene biggest hug you could ever imagine.

Jake and Jason Greene did not notice the events going on, their attention had been taken by the usual drama of getting the boys into their respective vehicles, kissing both Emma and Shireen Greene on the forehead whispered" Thanks".

Feeling left out of the group hug Sally Greene proceeded with haste to be a participant in this group hug, Emma and

Shireen stroked Marcus Greene's arm then made their way to the minibus, Sally Greene hugged Marcus Greene and said:" I'm not blind, I can see that it's times like this that can make any person feel lonely and cold, remember one thing Marcus Greene you are never on your own".

Sally Greene then kissed Marcus Greene on the cheek, held his arm, as they walked towards everyone else, Jake Greene with a cheeky smile said" Aye, Aye, what have you been up to with my wife" before Jake Green could finish his innuendo that everyone knew was about to arrive from his lips, Sally Greene said " Marcus and I are plotting to run away unless you buck up your ideas" Jason Greene burst out laughing with that Emma Greene turned to Jason Greene and commented, " I don't know what you are laughing at, you are on notice as well ". Both Jason and Jake looked at each, Marcus Greene stood smiling like a Cheshire cat, Sally and Emma Green hugged each other,

Sally said to Emma "Always a pleasure" Emma replied, "It sure is, coffee next week, we can decide if these two have been good, we can decide if we are going to run away with Marcus". Marcus Greene stood looking bemused, looked at his brothers and said: "You better be good boys ".

Everyone got into their cars Marcus Greene went to each car and said goodbye, waving to each car as they pulled away, Shireen pulled her phone to her face with a couple of tears ready to flood from her eyes, thinking how lonely it must be for her uncle, Emma Greene pulled a tissue out of her bag, trying to hold back the tears that wanted to escape from her eyes, said to Jason Greene and said " You are very lucky to have two good brothers, especially Marcus" Jason Greene replied in a sombre voice "I do feel a lucky man have two good brothers, I don't think I could be as tough but still caring as Marcus" Jason Greene went onto say" It's times like this you realise you should be grateful for the lives we do have "Emma Greene nodded in agreement, the same conversation took place took part with Sally and Jake Greene with the same tearful results.

The journey home was the usual of Harry and George being oblivious to their surroundings, like most young boy's fantasy action figures and superheroes arethe main topics, Emma and Jason Greene were in deep conversation about when the patio would be finally finished, which had the ultimatum of finish it or else,

Shireen's ride home that was something else entirlely, in deep thought about her transition from being from sitting in a pub to being in an alien world, which left her with a mixture of unexplained sights and feelings, totally memorised, excitement, scared, you name it, she was feeling it, experiencing those feelings just left her even more bewildered, making her wanting more of the same scared excited anticipation.

Emma Greene announced that they are going to be stopping at the supermarket, Shireen though it was the perfect time for a visit to the phone shop in store, like a commanding officer Emma Greene had everything planned, the plan just needs to be executed, as they arrived at the supermarket everyone exited the minibus, lined up in some sort of a line, like a dog's hind leg, Emma Greene then went up down the line, Emma Greene issued her orders like a good army officer, "Jason, you can take Harry and George to the toy department next to the electrical department", Jason Greene thought a result T.V.'s, football, fantastic, Emma Greene then informed Jason Greene" If the boys go missing in action, I will be sitting in the minibus and reading a magazine until you have found them both, understand".

Jason and the boys looked at each other, they realised that if they didn't get this right, there could be serious problems ahead for all of them, Emma Greene turned to Shireen and said "No need to ask where you want to go, mmmm let me think, phone shop maybe" Shireen just laughed, Emma Greene then said " When I ring you, it's all hands on deck for packing of the shopping bags" Jason Greene thought it would be funny to give a little salute, with Harry and George following in their father's stupidity, earned them look of unbelievable, then a shake of disbelieve from Emma Greene.

Everyone parted in various directions, Jason, Harry and George Greene practising the hundred-metre sprint towards supermarket entrance, Emma and Shireen Greene collected the shopping trolley, Emma and Shireen parted company with the words from Emma Greene" See you in a bit, "Shireen made straight for the mobile phone to drool over the latest mobiles, Shireen spotted her dream phone, staring and glaring not forgetting the wishing.

Conspiring on how she could convince her parents to part with cash for this mobile phone, she then heard a Faint voice with what she thought was her uncle's voice, her visions became hazy and somewhat misty, as she started to gain her eyesight from a blinding white haze and a brilliant white light, a vast breeze seemed to surround as she appeared to be in a never-ending tube that was immersed in darkness from the outside, inside them, there was a sheer white light on the inside, there was constant strobe of what can only be described as white gold lightning ran down the tube. Shireen could not decide whether she was travelling up or down on a cushion of air inside of this test tube surrounding tube.

Out of nowhere another tube of the same description appeared in a blinding flash, inside the other tube there was a mist, as the mist started to disappear there was an outline of a female, as the mist dissipated more and more, the female form pushed her hands against the tube when the mist finally cleared revealing what can only be described as an identical clone of Shireen, in excitement, fear and a mixture of all sorts of emotions, Shireen extended both arms and hands out. They made contact through the walls of the tubes, the texture of the tubes had a feeling that Shireen had never experienced before, the clone smiled then uttered the words softly " Don't be scared Shireen" as the clone went to say something else, feeling a vibration from her phone, Shireen's phone began to ring, shaking her head bringing her back to the world she recognised, Shireen answered her phone still somewhat bewildered "Hello", then came Emma

Greene's voice "Shireen, till four time to pack the shopping bags".

Shireen made her way to checkout four started considering these visions that kept occurring, what they meant, was she going insane, are they visions or even premonitions of the future, the fact that she kept hearing her uncle's voice was causing some anxiety and confusion, it was only the reassurance of Marcus Greene's voice that kept her thinking that she was going insane.

Shireen thought to herself could she talk to her mum about these visions, definitely not she thought to herself, Shireen just concluded that the voice of Marcus Greene had already said that time would reveal all, it is all a waiting game she concluded in her mind, a waiting game that was causing anxiety, excitement, frustration, complete multitude feelings as a young female was left bewildered.

All she wondered how many how frequent would these visions would occur, arriving at checkout four was next in the queue, Emma Greene noticed Shireen then said "Just in time, have you seen your father and brothers ?" with that there was a commotion coming towards checkout four, it was an argument between Jason Greene and his sons about how the referee needed to visit an optician, with Harry informing his father that he was a sore loser and cough up his winnings on the two pounds that they had coming, Jason Greene produced the two-pound owed, with smirk and code sending voice said "Thanks Dad", Emma Greene then gave her orders who was packing what items handing everyone a bag each.

Emma Greene paid the cashier then said "Let's go", as the Greene family are about to exit the store, Shireen heard her uncle's voice " Shireen don't be scared embrace your feelings, explore your visions, guidance will be at hand sooner than you think", as soon as Marcus Green's voice appeared out of nowhere it disappeared as in the same fashion, her body and mind were experiencing heightened emotions, all she wanted to do was to communicate with her uncle, Shireen thought to herself there will be a time and there will be a place.

Everyone placed their designated bags in the back of the minibus and took their usual seats, that's when Shireen started receiving messages from her friends saying what a crap day they had, she thought could she trust friends and confide in them, she then thought to herself, if I tell my friends what has happened today they won't believe me, furthermore they will assume I've lost the plot, Shireen thought best policy is to say nothing, texting back to her friends saying that her day had turned out better than anticipated, being proud of her new presents had to rub it in, knowing full well her friends would be jealous, it would be rude not too.

As the Greene family neared home Emma Greene announced that she couldn't be bothered to cook or even do sandwiches, that they are all going to have a Chinese takeaway, then announced which startled Jason Greene that he was paying for the takeaway, Emma Greene then said to Jason Greene "Don't forget my bottle of rose'", that made Jason Greene smile with delight, Emma Greene then turned to Shireen and her brothers and said "No individual orders, set meal for four , like it or lump it".

Finally arriving home there was a scramble to exit the minibus, Emma Greene waited for the scramble to finish, finally making an entrance at the front door turned to Harry and George and said, " No one can do anything else until the shopping has been put away", all the bags had been taken from the minibus, Jason Greene then proceeded to collect their Chinese takeaway order.

After all the shopping had been put away in their rightful places, Shireen could hear Jason Greene was manoeuvring his minibus in reverse into the drive, cutlery and plates, glasses and mugs, ended up in their rightful places, Jason Greene placed the takeaway order on the kitchen table, Emma Greene started de-bagging the take-away, then came the rush of the vultures, namely Harry and George, Emma Greene then placed a bit of everything onto everyone's plate.

Shireen just thought of the feeding time at the zoo scenario from this morning, deciding after finishing her meal that it was chillout time, message her friends, a bit of T.V. then fall asleep, not before there was a family effort to clean everything that was used for their meal.

When reaching her bedroom Shireen realised that she had forgotten her bracelets, so if she went reluctantly to retrieve her bracelets, after climbing the stairs back to her bedroom, she then thought time to get the messaging over and done with on social media, then it would be the usual T.V. shows, as Shireen closed her bedroom door, she could hear Harry and George being frog marched to the bathroom by her father, with both boys protesting that they are too tired to wash and clean their teeth, the orders had come from high command that under no exceptions, namely Emma Greene that her commands where to be obeyed.

After all the usual exhausted excuses had been made, Harry and George capitulated and went to bed, Harry then made a threat to Jason Greene that the N.S.P.C.C. would hear of their mistreatment, Child Line was also mentioned, Jason Greene replied to the threats and said" I will find the numbers for you in the morning" laughed and walked back downstairs laughing even more to himself at the exchange of comments, Shireen was also bemused at the exchange between her father and brothers.

After the usual social media banter and sending pictures of her presents, Shireen then decided to change ready for bed, bedside lamp on, T.V. on, flicking around the channels finally settling on a T.V. reality show, propped up on her pillows, started experiencing the drifting hazy feeling from early on in the day, a milky white haze formed in front of her eyes, as the haze started to clear, she then found herself looking at a beacon with the free-floating sphere, as from the earlier vision the beacon and sphere amazed her, shimmering white light flowing up and down the beacon extending to the sphere, with bursts of white bright energy flowing like lightning bolts flowing as fast as possible through the beacon and sphere, she then discovers herself standing next to what appears to be the length of what she has trouble to comprehend is a white horse.

Shireen is about to turn and pivot, to fully look at what she believes is a horse, when, what appears to be a pair of dragon's wings, start to emerge from the side of this white horse, the hoofs on this horse start to change into what can only be described as dragons' feet or some other creature like feet.

Shireen reluctantly starts to turn to look at the head of whatever this creature is about to become, as quickly as it happened, the experience of this vision or whatever you want to call it finished, not sure what she should be feeling at that precise moment, whether it should be frustrating on not finding out what the outcome of the full transformation of this creature, she thought to herself, should she be grateful that the vision or whatever you want to call it finished when it did, the experience certainly exhausted Shireen, one thing she knew a deep and meaning conversation was required with her uncle Marcus.

As Shireen slept and dreamt her dreams of happiness, a woman's voice starting calling to her, she recognised the woman's voice, her dreams starting drifting into another dimension, she found herself in the courtyard of what looked like a large Tudor style palace, the woman that was calling Shireen had her back to her, dressed in what can only be described as some sort of black ninja outfit with thigh-high leather boots, the woman raised her left hand into the air producing a coin in her hand.

Shireen could not see what the coin was in this woman's hand, as she tried to squint and see what was on the coin, the thought of could this be the coin that her uncle Marcus had given her entered Shireen's brain, also was this the same coin that was exchanged with sexy Sandra at the church fete for the bracelets.

As Shireen tried to walk towards this woman, it seemed she

that her progress was being hindered, one step forward, three steps backwards, this is when she could only see the outline of the woman, the woman turned around and waved then walked away, Shireen furiously strained her eyes to try and have a glimpse of this woman's face, her frustrated efforts produced nothing.

Waking-up , shook her head, trying to remember her dream, vision, with frustration, totally vexed by her situation, Shireen fumbled around for her phone, ready to call her uncle then looked at her bedside clock and realised it was three-thirty am and not the best of times to call her uncle Marcus, looking for her headphones, she found her headphones just underneath her bed , putting her headphones on and tried to relax with some music but the thoughts of her encounter just kept on returning to haunt her.

Finally falling into a deep sleep, Shireen kept having a reoccurring dream of her encounter with the ninja dressed woman with the thigh-high leather boots, Shireen ran and ran after this woman, this unknown person kept increasing her distance until Shireen could no longer have visual sight of this female, finding herself so exhausted Shireen fell into such deep sleep that anything she dreamt of became insignificant due to her tiredness.

It was about 5:30 am when Shireen stirred from her sleep needing to use the bathroom, she lifted her weary head from her pillows, as she returned from the bathroom, the box containing her bracelets attracted her attention, the box started to stream sunbeams of light through the edges of the box, picking up the box with hesitation she opened the box, as she opened the box to expose the bracelets to her eyes, her room lit up as if was it was hit by a furious bolt of lightning, this blinding light sent back to the courtyard of the Tudor looking palace, where she first encountered the woman in the ninja type uniform with the thigh high leather boots, the difference this time she was looking down at herself in a ninja type uniform with the tight leather boots, on this uniform at the top of her left arm there is the emblem of the beacon and the floating sphere, raising her head looking straight at this beacon and sphere had glowing white realms of light going through the beacon and sphere, then was an almighty lightning strike, the bolt of lightning striking first the sphere melting right through the sphere like a knife going through soft butter, the bolt of lightning then impacted into the top of the beacon cascading right through the beacon disappearing to whatever below ground ,this was an incredible site ,totally confused Shireen went racing towards the beacon but the inevitable happened, finding herself back in her bedroom, Shireen's frustration was gaining momentum with intensity with each vision that she encounters.

By this time tiredness set in as Shireen fell back onto her bed with exhaustion, finally feeling of some sort satisfaction from her latest vision, at least her visions are starting to form some sort of pattern of a jigsaw, the only frustration is that some of the important pieces of the jigsaw had not presented them self's, the problem from Shireen's perspective is that she felt that having half a jigsaw left her in a quagmire, the feeling of the jigsaw parts from the box, did leave Shireen frustrated in no uncertain terms, she then thought about her possible phone conversation with her uncle Marcus, realising that if she tried to have an in-depth conversation with her uncle could achieve less than rather than achieve more, the fact of the matter that Shireen concluded, uncle Marcus was correct, that time would reveal all, time would explain everything.

Shireen started to realise that she was starting a transformation from an adolescent into a young woman, the feeling of a radical change her personality, the feeling of being more aware of her emotions and a radical change in her perspective of life, she even started to think the entire way she looked, presented herself, behaved in every aspect of her personality may need a total transformation, thinking to herself one day at a time, maybe it was time to say goodbye to the old Shireen and well come the new Shireen with open arms.

Contemplating her next action of a strategy that she had in mind to try and have an extra couple of hours sleep, realising that would not happen soon as her delightful brothers awake from their delightful dreams, slaying zombies and any other creatures they could think up in their creative minds was their idea of a good night's sleep.

Sunday was Sunday in the Greene household, Jason Greene was being a good boy, up early did whatever Emma Greene requested without any protests or excuses,

Emma Greene knew exactly why there was a keenness to please and do anything she requested, Football, Jason Greene was aiming to go and watch his favourite team playing lunchtime first match of the afternoon, Emma Greene turned to Jason Greene and informed him "Don't forget my parents are coming to lunch" with a sheepish grin said, " What time is lunch going to be?" Emma Greene hands-on-hips said "Why, "Emma Greene knew what was coming, just wanted some pleasure and entertainment of seeing Jason Greene plead his case for going to the pub.

Emma Greene replied "3 pm, I know why you asking, these are the ground rules" Jason Greene looking with apprehension nodded in agreeance, Emma Greene when onto say" You finish the peeling the potatoes, the veg, the shopping list is on the table, my dad will be coming with you", Jason Greene had a good rapport with his father-in-law Carl, bit hesitant with his mother-in-law Sue, as Jason Greene knew she was the one person you didn't mess with, just like her dear daughter.

Emma Greene added a couple of other things to her list of demands" Don't forget a bottle of rose' for me and mum, don't my mother will be picking you at 3 pm prompt, be outside, you know what the consequences will be", Jason Greene thought result, Jason Greene set the alarm on his phone for 2:55 pm as fouling this up is not an option.

At about 10 pm Harry and George thought it would be immense fun to burst into Shireen's room to jump on her bed, as they tried to burst and force their way into Shireen's room, they bounced off the door into a heap on the floor, what they hadn't realised after many protests from their sister, Jason Greene had fitted a lock to his daughter's bedroom door, Shireen opened her door laughed at the sight of Harry and George in a heap with a cheeky smile said" Did you Knock", George replied "What happened there?",

Shireen smirked and said" I will tell you what happened there, you got caught out, that's what's happened", Shireen just closed and locked her door.

Emma Greene called up the stairs "Breakfast is now, move your backsides", Harry and George flew down the stairs like a couple of banshee's, sternly manner Shireen flowed down the stairs in blue jogging bottoms and top, already at the table sat the brothers Grimm, slapping and kicking each other until Emma Greene flicked their ears and said in a firm and demanding voice" Enough", Harry and George knew not to proceed with their altercation on one another, this would result in harsh punishment, NO PLAY STATION OR X-BOX, as the boys settled down to their cereal. Shireen made an entrance and commented, "Feeding time at the chimps' enclosure ", Harry and George made it quite clear that they did not like Shireen's comments, the response from Harry and George involved a disgruntled look and the poking of tongues out at Shireen.

Shireen then waltzed passed her brothers giving them a sibling show of affection, flicking their ears and mentioning those immortal words" Is Dumbo aware you have his ears and his spare pair by the looks of it",

Before things escalated into a full-blown war of words, Emma Greene interrupted and proceeded to say" Not this morning, not today, Grandad John and Grandma Sue are coming to lunch, so it's all hands on deck", everyone then realised the seriousness of the situation, Shireen made her toast, had her cup of tea, the boys just thought pocket money, Jason Greene arrived home from his Sunday expedition to the supermarket, Emma Greene advised Jason

Greene" Go and make yourself pretty and make yourself smell nice, you need to go and pick my parents up", Jason Greene thought football time is looming fast.

Shireen sat down to eat her toast, drank her tea, then flew like an eagle after its prey up the stairs to her bedroom, grabbed a towel and dressing gown, straight into the bathroom, Harry and George making themselves look adorable in their bedroom, the result would be pocket money from Grandma Sue, Jason Greene looking presentable grabbed his minibus keys kissed Emma Greene on the cheek, jumped in his minibus and off he went.

Emma Greene stood back in the kitchen, that is everything done, time to get ready for her guests, everything was working like clockwork, which is a first in the Greene household, as Emma Greene reached the top of the stairs the bathroom door opened, Shireen exited the bathroom leaving it free for Emma Greene to have a quick shower, put her clothes on, do her and hair and make-up.

The military exercise, operation GET READY, was a great success; any military commander would have been proud of the co-ordination and timing.

As everyone stood to attention to be inspected by Emma Greene, everyone got the once over, verbal commands were issued, consequences and punishments of non-compliance were conveyed, just at that moment the engine of Jason Greene's minibus could be heard, Emma Greene opened the front door, Harry and George went to greet their grandparents.

Shireen said to her brothers "Thanks for coming, do call again", as her brothers stepped outside the front door, then the customary greetings took place, Jason Greene waited in anticipation for the all-clear from Emma Greene to take himself and his father-in-law to his local, before Emma Greene could utter a word Jason Greene's mother-in-law gave a few words of wisdom, turning to her husband John and Jason Greene said "Gentlemen, 3 pm on the dot or else", both males nodded in agreeance, smiled to each other, proceeded like Ghurkha platoon on a quick forced march, Emma Greene opened the fridge and said to her mum" Rose' or tea?", Emma's mum grinned and said, "My dear girl, I think you know what's appropriate".

As the wine was flowing from the bottle into the glasses, Shireen made an entrance, Shireen looked at her mum and grandma before Shireen could say anything Emma Greene said to her daughter " One glass for you Shireen and that's it ".

Shireen now felt part of the official womanhood group, Shireen has a nagging Question for both her mum and grandma, plucking up the courage asked her question,

Looking at her mum and grandma said," Why was I named Shireen? who thought of the name Shireen?", Emma Greene looked at her mum, took a sip from her glass and said," Mother I think I will let you answer that one",

Emma's mum said " Thank you for that my dear", Emma's mum informed Shireen, It was her uncle, Marcus who presented the name to everyone, as Emma and Jason Greene could not agree on a name for you when you were born, Shireen then asked" What does it mean? where does name Shireen come from ?", Shireen's grandma replied holding Shireen's hand said" It is a Persian stroke Indian name, it means sweet, pleasant, gentle, delicate", after taking a sip of wine from her glass went onto say "It was your uncle Marcus who thought of your name".

Shireen thought to herself, why doesn't this surprise me, Shireen's grandma said, "Don't you like the name?"

Shireen replied " I love the name, just I've been curious about the origins and the meaning of my name for a while.

Well, it was all hands on deck, Harry and George laid out the table settings, Shireen, Emma Greene and grandma put everything to cook for lunch, Shireen decided to sit in the garden and reflect on the influence that her uncle Marcus had on her life, he had more of an influence than Shireen could imagine, time flew that lunchtime before Shireen could collect her thoughts of the weekend and her visions or dreams of what may be the future, came the ultimate call of " Lunch is ready", on the button Jason Greene and father-in-law appeared very happy with the result of their football team outside the pub just as their taxi pulled up making it on time for lunch.

After their beef lunch came homemade apple crumble and custard, everyone settled down in the back garden as it was a pleasant day, Harry and George played the adorable grandchildren ensure pocket money would be paid, Shireen sat on the sun lounger near her brothers swings, her mind started to wander, a cascade of thoughts ran through her mind about the visions she had, whether they would come true and in what order, the obligatory pocket money was paid out, before everyone had realised 5 pm had arrived and it was time for Shireen's grandparent's to leave and go home, dead on time the taxi turned up, everyone had their hugs and kisses. The Greene family stood outside and waved to the taxi as it pulled away.

Sunday night meant bath night for Shireen and her siblings, the usual fuss came from Harry and George, Shireen watched T.V. multi-tasked talking to her friends on social media, Shireen had her shower, checked her homework for school the next day, she decided there was nothing of interest on T.V. put her headphones on, loaded up some chillout music and relaxed.

Deep in thought again Shireen was trying to contemplate if and when she was going to indulge in any more visions while asleep, as the music relaxed Shireen, she drifted into a sleep that was so delightful that her whole body just felt like she was drifting on a white fluffy cloud, that seemed to be on a gentle breeze raising up and then lowering down, creating a most easing and massaging feeling on her body.

Shireen opened her eyes, all she could see is a blue sky, with white clouds surrounding Shireen, you just wanted to jump and down on these heavenly clouds, some objects or creatures flew and soared directly over Shireen, these objects or creatures or however you wanted to describe this entity, were invisible to the naked eye, they had a cloaking device, they only manifested to one's eyes when a rush of energy would filter right through this mystical creature, like a wave rolling from the sea, occasionally there would be a rush of fast lightning bolts cascading throughout this creature revealing it's magnificence to Shireen.

The feeling that Shireen had just witnessed a magical moment as she drifted on a cushion of air enthralled her, a haze then descended over Shireen's eyes sending her back to her bedroom in a daze, back to surroundings of familiarity.

Shireen woke up looked at her alarm clock, looking at the time of 3:55 am did not impress her at all, giving an extreme tearful yawn she drifted back to sleep, Shireen fought with dreams that she dreamt tossing and turning, living each segment of her premonitions that she had encountered throughout the weekend, which left Shireen addicted to her possible future, wanting more parts of the visionary jigsaw to appear. Shireen struggled furiously on occasions trying to make the parts of her visionary jigsaw to fall into place, only to make her dreaming vexing and perplexing, Shireen finally found solace at 4:30 am in the dream of earlier premonition, drifting, floating aimlessly looking at the blue sky surrounded by the most inviting clouds, the creature that Shireen encountered became more visible, the strobes of cascading light intensified when flowing from one end of the creature to the other side of this unknown entity, followed by pulsating bursts of lightning made it the most eye addictive collage of colours that anyone could imagine.

CHAPTER THREE
ANTICIPATION

Emma Greene stretched when the 6:30 alarm activated, yawning and preparing herself for the Monday morning onslaught of pre-planned military operation code name

:OPERATION SCHOOL RUN: the following orders were issued to Jason Greene, kids out of bed, "make sure they wash and brush their teeth", this comment was mainly aimed at Harry and George as they would go to school looking like a pair of waifs and strays, As Jason planted a kiss on Emma Greene lips, Emma Greene then said to Jason Greene " your sandwiches in the fridge "Jason Greene said "What would I do without you" Emma Greene replied " Starve probably", as everyone made their attempts to drag themselves from the last of whatever dreams that lingered in their minds, Shireen's alarm discharged it's grating piercing on the ears sound, Shireen held out her limp right arm to turn her alarm off, deciding that Monday was not going away dragged herself out of bed, passing her father as he entered her siblings bedroom, Saturdays episode of the bathroom scene repeated itself, Harry tried to push pass Shireen, Shireen then pushed Harry to one side flicking his right ear in the process, Harry's response again to the ear flicking" That hurt" Shireen's response in her own loving way "It was meant to".

Emma Greene watched the incident said to Shireen" If you keep doing that your brother is going to have the same matching ears as dumbo", Both Shireen and her mum gave a little giggle, Shireen looked at her mum and nodded in agreeance, after Shireen's bathroom time was over and made her way back to her bedroom, her favourite time of the morning was looming, breakfast with her brothers, putting the final touches to her hair and uniform, Shireen looked into her full length and wondered what Monday had in store for her.

Shireen grabbed her backpack as she did she found herself in a different realm, back in what she called a travel tube that glowed like a sunbeam, Shireen just hung in a warm relaxing floating cloud, out of nowhere like a bolt of lightning from the gods, when Shireen finally regained her eyesight from being blinded from this heavenly bolt from above, there in front of Shireen with arms and hands stretched out was her clone, she made contact by stretching her arms then hands out, finally making contact with the palms of their hands, Shireen's clone talked to Shireen through telepathy whispering the words "Shireen don't afraid, embrace your destiny, you have the fortitude, your beauty can subdue anything or anyone, Shireen you have been chosen, time is near and you must decide if you want to be chosen.

As quickly as her travel to what can be called as a travel tube happened, Shireen found herself back in her bedroom still clutching her backpack, Emma Greene soon snapped Shireen out of her trance by calling "Shireen, come on, otherwise, we are going to be late",she soon fled down the stairs straight into the front seat of her mother's car, Shireen put on her seat belt, Emma Greene started her car turned to Shireen and said "Nice of you to join us", both had a little chuckle, Emma Greene then put her car into gear and made her way to Nusea junior school to drop off Harry and George, the usual banter between siblings took place with the odd threats of retribution and reprisals, To ignore her dear brothers Shireen turned up the car radio not to hear her brothers, Emma Greene turned the volume of the car radio back down to a reasonable level.

On arrival at Nusea Junior school, Harry and George clambered out of the car with the mandatory Bye mum", before Emma Greene could utter any words Harry and George had disappeared into a swarm of other children, Emma Greene turned to Shireen and said" Right missy your turn", Shireen looked at her mum said with disillusioned face with sad puppy eyes "Do I have to go to school today it's only a revision day", Emma Greene replied "Today is my time day, the answer is no Shireen, that look might work with your father but it won't work with me", replied "Please mum", Emma Greene insisted with the word "No", Emma Greene pulled into Nusea secondary modern school, Shireen with disappointment on her face opened the car door looked at a her mum with a despondent voice said "Bye mum", Emma Greene replied" Enjoy" then sped away turning up her favourite song on her C.D. player, Shireen walked towards her registration class, bumping into her friends Sophie and Clara,Clara was about five foot four slim build Jet black hair had that Spanish look about her, Sophie on the other hand was of average build five foot six tall, all had the same look on their faces of life is unfair, Clara said to Shireen luck like us staying home to do revision, simultaneously both Shireen and said" Nope", the three girls just burst out laughing, the registration bell rung out all three girls agreed that they would try and sit together in the revision hall.

As Shireen fumbled into her registration class, then escaped as quickly as possible to the revision hall meeting up with Sophie and Clara, Clara was very organised she had obtained for all three of them to go to the library to do their revision, more like natter about the weekend's events and trivial matters not relating in the slightest to any schoolwork.

All three sat at the very back of the library where a small interview room was situated, this was now occupied by the three girls, The first words spoken by any of the three girls came from Sophie," Let's see them" to Shireen, with the response of "What" came from Shireen, Sophie replied "Your presents silly" the three girls laughed, Shireen reached into the top of her opened blouse and proceed to pull out her chain with the pendant on the chain, Shireen took the pendant of so it could be passed around her two friends, Clara piped up and said" Now the bracelets "reluctantly Shireen pulled out the box containing the bracelets slowly opened the box to reveal the two bracelets, the window at the back of the library was hit by a bolt of brilliant sunlight, forcing it's way through the window exploding onto the bracelets this bolt of sunlight when hitting the bracelets produced a dazzling multitude of colours memorised the three girls, like looking through a kaleidoscope of hypnotising colours.

All three girls gasped with amazement, excited with what they had just witnessed gave a "WOW", closing the box placing it back safely in her backpack, Clara uttered the words "Absolutely beautiful Shireen "Sophie was just gobsmacked, all Sophie could do is a nod in agreeance, speechless for a moment or two said to Shireen "You are so lucky", Shireen gave a cheesy smile and said, "I sure am".

With the usual gossiping incorporated with the interruption of studying, morning breaks and lunchtime made the day glide with ease for Shireen and friends.

With five minutes to escape home time, Shireen, Clara and Sophie loaded up their books, bits and pieces and made their way to perspective rides home, parting company at the pick-up lay-by gave their hugs goodbye, waving goodbye to her friends, Shireen opened the front door to her mum's car to her amazement no brothers, Emma Greene could see the joyous look on Shireen's face, before she could make and produce a comment from her mouth, Emma Greene with a big grin on her face said to Shireen "Your dad is picking up your brothers for football practice", Emma Greene started her car, put her indicator on pulled away from the school, Shireen was a bit confused as they did not seem to be going in the direction of home.

Shireen said with a puzzled look and voice said to her mum "Where are we going", Emma Greene replied "Well, I've had a tax rebate, me and you are going for a coffee and a bit of retail therapy", Both daughter and mother parted an ear-shattering "YES", arriving at NuSea town centre Emma Greene parked her car, both Shireen and Emma Greene exited the car, Shireen putting her backpack into the boot of the car, Emma and Shireen made their way to the nearest coffee shop, Shireen found a vacant table by the front window, Emma Greene went and gave their order, paid, sat down by Shireen, with a, I don't know how expression on Shireen's face "Mum, I don't know that much about uncle Marcus", Emma Greene looked at Shireen with anticipation of what's coming next expression, Shireen further added to her question "What can you tell me about him?", Emma Greene replied with a question of her own "Why the sudden interest", Shireen wanting to blurt out about her visions, premonitions, managed to stop herself at the last moment, Shireen answered her mother with "My curiosity has got the better of me, uncle Marcus seems different to dad and uncle Jake", Emma Greene knew exactly what Shireen was trying to express to her, wanting to see what Shireen would convey to her just said "You mean like chalk and cheese", Shireen straight away sat upright and replied "Yes, that's right, I know he has had various jobs, before opening his shop", before anything else could be said a waitress appeared with their order of two latte's, followed by two slices of lemon drizzle cake.

Emma Greene opened two packets of brown sugar , poured them into her latte, stirred her latte and said "You know your uncle was in the army, what you don't know he was in military intelligence, he done ok for himself, rising to the rank of warrant officer class one", Shireen's face was a picture, looking shelled shocked said to her mum, just said in amazement "WOW", Emma Greene pleaded with Shireen, with a hesitant voice, knowing someday Shireen would know the truth said "Promise me this Shireen this goes know further, otherwise your father will divorce me and your uncle would not speak to me again", Shireen nodded agreeing to her mother's terms, Emma Greene went onto say "your uncle was deemed by some teachers at his school that he would not amount to anything, your father will tell you that some teachers where useless that's why there was a major investigation into the school", Shireen looked flabbergasted, Emma Greene gathered her thoughts and carried on with what she was saying "On leaving school your uncle tried a few jobs, then decided to join the army at eighteen", pausing to take a bite of her cake and a sip from her mug of latte, carried on "Within six years rising to the rank of staff sergeant, in uniform chest full of medals went to a school reunion ten years later, the teachers who said he would not achieve anything in life had to eat their words", Shireen butted in and said "What did uncle Marcus say to them", Emma Greene gave a little smile, replied "Your uncle said nothing, had a cup of tea, looked each one of them in the eyes, then a teacher by the name of Xander Blackstone, your uncle had a lot of respect for this teacher,walked towards your uncle, stopped, looked directly into your uncles eyes and said quietly,"you have made your point good boy, please go Marcus,I understand why you had to prove to this school it's failings, why you had to attend this reunion to seek justification and clarification on your new found status ,anything else will spoil what you have achieved tonight", he hasn't been back to that school since the reunion".

Pausing to finish her cake, take another sip of latte, Emma Greene carried on with what she was saying to Shireen "Well, time went by, your uncle got married, two years before retirement your uncle went on a hush, hush mission.

Before Emma Greene could complete her story, the coffee shop door opened and a familiar voice said "Two cappuccinos' to go please", Emma Greene and Shireen automatically looked at this man at the counter, It was Marcus Greene, Emma Greene said in a joking tone in her voice "Marcus Greene, too many of those and your waist band will be on critical", Emma Greene and Shireen could not contain their laughter, Marcus Greene spun around recognising those dulcet tones of Emma Greene's voice, saw Shireen and Emma Greene and made his way to their table, pulled a chair out from under the table, sat down, looked at Shireen and Emma Greene with an ecstatic smile said "Two princesses I am so happy to see, let me guess why you are in town this afternoon "leaning over grabbed a tea towel a waitress had left on the adjoining table, Marcus Greene put the tea towel over his head and pretending to a fortune teller, indulged in a bit of role-play, rubbing an imaginary crystal ball said "I see you have come into some money, retail therapy is going to play a part in this afternoon's proceedings", Emma Greene crunching up her face trying not laugh, Shireen just turned away laughed with embarrassment, then turning back to her uncle with a smile from ear to ear, Emma Greene knew that her brother-in-law had been talking to his brother, in a voice of bemusement said "Funny, very funny, obviously you have been talking to your brother "Marcus Greene gave a hearty laugh, Emma Greene said jokingly "Your brother will pay dearly for this", Shireen interrupted and said to her uncle "Well done, bravo, Oscars this time next year", before anybody could indulge in any other conversation the waitress call over to say Marcus Greene's order was ready, leaving the table said "Ladies always a pleasure to see you".

Emma Greene replied "The same here", Shireen replied "Lovely to see you uncle Marcus", as Marcus Greene picked up his order of two cappuccino's, about to leave the coffee shop, Emma Greene called to Marcus Greene and said "Marcus, curry night on Wednesday, I'm not taking no for an answer", Marcus Greene just smiled, knowing he couldn't get out of curry night even if he tried, Emma Greene went on to say "Jason will call you with the details", Marcus Greene just smirked and said knowing he had been beaten said "Ok, see you then", he then opened up the coffee shop door and made his way back to his emporium, Shireen thought to herself, Wednesday might be the exact opportunity she was looking for to obtain some answers from her uncle.

Shireen and her mum finished their latte's said their thank you to the staff, both mother and daughter left the coffee shop, perused around a few shops, buying a thing here and there, Shireen came across the local martial arts shop, in the window was a cardboard cut-out in what appears to be a girl in a ninja outfit holding a Tachi Samurai sword, all of a sudden Shireen felt as if she was being sucked from one world to the next in a blink of an eye, Shireen found herself in front of herself, was she looking at herself or was it her clone she came into contact earlier in her visions , black ninja outfit thigh hi leather boots, holding a sword similar to a Wakizashi Samurai machete in her right hand, in her left hand was an identical weapon of a Wakizashi Samurai Machete, the blades on these fearsome swords did not shine, the colour of the blades where a copper blood red with traditional binding on the handles, the a final interesting touch was an emblem of the beacon of light where the copper blood-red blade met the handle.

Realising it was the clone that stood in front of her, the clone whispered to Shireen "Soon", as quickly as the vision entered her head, it exited in the manner.

Shireen regained her senses with the cardboard cut still in front her through the shop window, Shireen turned to see her mum making her way towards her, peering over her shoulder Emma Greene said in a humorous tone" Like that type of thing do you "Emma Greene nudged her daughter, mother and daughter turned and looked at each other giggling, Emma Greene said"Right, lets grab a burger, then home "Shireen gave a nod and a smile, with a couple of shop stops on the way to their burger, Emma Greene strolled up to the counter while Shireen found a table, Shireen made herself comfortable not long afterwards joined by her mum, with hardly anybody being in the burger bar Shireen pursed the conversation from earlier, she then plucked up the courage and said

" Mum, Uncle Marcus, you didn't finish your story about him", Emma Greene knew this subject would rear its head again, rather she feared it would not be forgotten, in an understanding voice, knowing Shireen's frustration said "Look, Shireen, I've said to much already, let's us say he was a very brave man, I'm sure if you ask him what he had achieved, where he had served and what he did, he will release the information he would like you to know, when he feels the time is appropriate " Shireen protested and tried to understand her mother's reluctance to divulge any more information, Emma Greene held Shireen's hand, Shireen said "I can understand what you mean, I won't tell anyone", Emma Greene looked at Shireen in a sympathetic expression still holding Shireen's hand said" I'm not saying that you will say anything intentionally, there may be an occasion you may forget yourself, I can't afford to give any more information, I'm sorry that's the way it is", Shireen looking at her mother's point of view, just smiled and replied, I understand", Emma Greene was so relieved at Shireen's response, the last thing Emma Greene wanted is to fallout with her daughter.

Emma Greene and Shireen finished the remains of their meal, then picked up their shopping bags, made their way to the front of the burger bar, then strolling down the shopping mall giggling and laughing at anything that wasn't of a serious nature in their eyes, passing the martial arts shop Shireen glanced over quickly, remembering her vision wondering to herself how long is soon, how many visions before the truth would expose itself, time will tell is the expression which is most appropriate Shireen thought to herself, then carried on with her conversation with her mother.

Shireen enjoyed the afternoon bonding with her mum, although Emma Greene wouldn't spill the beans on Marcus, her uncle, proved one thing to Shireen, that Emma Greene was not only a truly amazing mum but a true confident, Shireen struggled on the way home to confide in her mum about her visions, knowing that it might ask too many questions, Shireen clasped Emma Greene's and said "Thank you", Emma Greene didn't question Shireen's out of the blue expression of gratitude, only feeling a closer bond to her daughter, Emma Greene pulled into the Greene household drive, Collected their spoils from their shopping therapy, Emma Greene opened up the front door with Shireen closely behind her mum, Shireen and mum were greeted by a sheepish Jason Greene and sons all supporting bruises of conflict, Emma Greene said to Jason Greene "What the hell happened" Jason Greene in a bravado voice said" Our son made a tackle then the boy's father started on Harry, I stuck up for Harry and did what every father would have done", the aftermath resulted in Jason Greene and sons supporting facial bruises, the good news, the attacking parties came of worse, Emma Greene didn't know whether to feel proud of her husband or be annoyed for the injuries they had received, it was only when George the youngest of her children hugged his mum said "They started on us mum, we sorted it", with a mixture of emotions flowing Emma Greene hugged all of them, with Shireen following closely to mum shed a tear hugged everyone.

That night was pizza and antiseptic wash for the abrasions and bruises, after Shireen and siblings had made their way to bed, Emma Greene and Jason Greene settled down in front of the T.V.

Emma Greene snuggled into Jason Greene, they looked at each other, no words could convey their feelings, Jason Greene looked at Emma Greene and said "I have spoken with Marcus today, I will be looking forward to seeing him Wednesday, I owe him so much, well, we owe him so much, he believed in me, when others gave up on me", Jason Greene snuggled up to Emma Greene, Emma Greene said "Time for bed", Shireen Greene just settled down for bed wondering what tonight's dreams will bring her, dressed for bed, she sloped under her duvet, then it happened, the visionary jigsaw bombarded Shireen's mind, cascading from every direction came the visions, Shireen thrashed around in her bed like a horse that refused to be tamed, somewhere in the night Shireen found solace and easing of the mind, the voice of Marcus Greene entered Shireen's head, the voice of Marcus Greene echoed and said "The time is near, the choice is yours, the truth will reveal itself", she then became settled, the easing words of her uncle sent her into a deep relaxed sleep, that wasn't to last, with a blinding flash in her mind Shireen found herself high in the sky flying through the air, finding herself on the back of a creature that resembled the body of a horse with wings and the head of a dragon, the amazing thing that exhilarated Shireen, she embraced the experience of flying and gliding through the air on this creature so easily , Shireen no longer feared the experience of her visions instead she became totally enthralled.

The rush of the flight on this creature that myths you only read about in fantasy books came to an abrupt end, a severe blinding flash of brought Shireen back to the world and reality she knew, waking from her sleep, got out of her bed to use the bathroom, as she crossed the landing she noticed brightness of the kitchen light emit its way up the staircase, making her way downstairs, leant over the banister, peered through the crack of the kitchen door to see her father with a cup of coffee in hands. She saw the sullen look on her father's face, making the final steps down the staircase Shireen opened up the kitchen door, Jason Greene looked up from his coffee and said "Hi there, what are you doing up", Shireen looking at her father concerned for him said "I needed the bathroom noticed the kitchen light on", Shireen then to rub the back of father's shoulders, then said in a sympathetic voice" Dad are you ok?, you seem to have the weight of the world on your shoulders", Jason Greene half turned to look at Shireen, smiled, then tried reassure Shireen with the words "I'm fine thanks", clasping Shireen's hands as Jason Greene spoke his words, "Shireen not convinced by her father's words insisted and said "Dad, please be honest with me", before Jason Green could reply in any, shape or form, Emma Greene made an entrance through the Kitchen door and said "It's the third anniversary of Nan and Granddads Greene's death in two weeks", The Greene brothers lost their parents in a collision with a drunk driver on their way home late night shopping, Marcus Greene had not only stepped up as an older brother, Marcus had now inherited the role of surrogate parents to his brothers, at the untimely death of the Greene brothers parents ,trying to deal with his wife's terminal cancer of which she died of a year before the death of his parents, Marcus Greene took the challenges laid before him and executed his duties with resilience, fortitude, courage, understanding and kindness, while still reeling from his wife's demise Marcus Greene never denied his brothers his attention when they required it.

After Emma Greene's announcement in the kitchen, Shireen hugged her father, Emma Greene clutched her husband's hands then stroking his hands in reassurance, Emma Greene said" Marcus will be here Wednesday for a curry, he will put you back into sync", Jason Greene gave a little smile then replied to Emma Greene "Good old Marcus, I don't know how he does it, especially after all he has been through", Shireen pulled up a chair next to her father, before anybody could express any sort of opinion said to her parents "What makes uncle Marcus tick, he seems always to know what to say and when to say it", Jason Greene looked at Shireen and said "I suppose it's all down to life experiences and choices, knowing life goes on", Jason Greene further said, "When it comes to grief your uncle he grieves in private, biting his tongue to keep his emotions in check so he can be a strong pillar for the rest of us", at that point Emma Greene intervened and said "Right, group therapy is over, back to bed everyone", Emma Greene looked at the kitchen clock, the clock advertised the fact it was 4.15am, everyone put the kitchen chairs back in their rightful places, Jason Greene being last one to exit the kitchen turned off the light, climbing the stairs one after another entered their respective bedrooms Shireen just collapsed onto her bed, still with her dressing gown wrapped around her body just pulled her duvet over her weary body and mind, falling asleep just as her head hit the pillows on her bed.

The sun shone on Shireen's face realising it was morning reaching for her phone, Shireen picked up her phone, she then took a glance at her phone, then panicked when she realised it relayed the message to her brain with the time of 9.30 am, she drew back her duvet, put her slippers on went down stairs, went into the kitchen, Emma Greene said without turning her back said " fried egg rolls for breakfast, a stunned Shireen said "Mum it's 9.30 I'm late for school", Emma Greene looked back replied "Well, you have a revision week and we all didn't get back to bed until late", Shireen replied in a concerned and curious voice "How was dad this morning?, was he ok?", Emma Greene turned back and smiled at Shireen and said "Dad is ok ,just needs some TLC at the moment", in an inquisitive voice Shireen asked "What

51

about uncle Marcus, to, who's looking out for him?", Emma Greene sighed then said "We are going to look out for him, it's the least we can do", Shireen sat at the kitchen table to be greeted by two fried egg rolls with brown sauce and a cup of tea, Emma Greene sat opposite her daughter with her fried egg rolls and tea, Shireen said to her mum "Haven't you got work today, Emma Greene said "I'm owed some flexi-time so I've taken the rest of the week off", Emma Greene said to Shireen "You can help me with the shopping for the curry night tomorrow", Shireen just nodded in agreeance as she then bit into her fried egg roll, after everything was squared away Shireen had a quick shower then sat at her dressing table looked into her mirror, a mist obscured her eyes, as she regained her eyesight she could see that she was exiting a white cloud, travelling in flight on the back of the creature from a previous vision, the wind just flowed and glided through her hair and body, the creature took a sharp left hand dive then opened up its wings and soared like an eagle looking for its prey, Shireen found the experience exhilarating beyond all belief, the usual thing happened to Shireen, as quickly as she experienced her vision it disappeared in the same manner, Shireen had her moment of frustration that her vision didn't extend beyond the usual time limited experience.

Awakening from her vision the blistering sun that poked its way through the gaps of her bedroom curtains, stretching and yawning Shireen couldn't be bothered with her hair that morning and just put it in a pony tail, then call, the ultimate call of "Shireen, are you ready?",Shireen called back "Yes, just putting on my jeans", slipping on her black trainers, put the strap of her small tan handbag over her head, then grabbed her navy blue sweatshirt, Shireen looked in her full length mirror and said to herself "Looking good babe", then smiled and scurried down the stairs to be greeted by her mum, as Shireen and Emma Greene looked at each other, it was like looking at twins, both wearing white t-shirt, slightly faded jeans both wearing black trainers, only difference Emma Greene had a beige handbag and light grey sweatshirt.

Emma Greene greeted Shireen at the bottom of the stairs, looking Shireen up and down, grinned and said "Like two peas in a pod, it's going to be me and mini me today", both Shireen and Emma Greene burst out laughing, Shireen locked the front door As Emma Greene reversed her car out of the drive, opening up the front passenger door Shireen flung her bag on to the back seat of the car and then her sweatshirt also ended up on the back seat of the car, then she closed the her door, put her seatbelt on, turned on the radio, Emma Greene turned to Shireen then said "Right, change of plan", Shireen gave her mum a confused look and said "How do you mean mum?", Emma Greene replied in an assertive voice "Tomorrows curry night is for uncle Marcus's birthday", Shireen sunk in her seat with embarrassment, Shireen had forgotten about her uncle's birthday, Emma Greene continued with "I'm not going to cook, we are going to Something Nice Indian restaurant, I've already informed your father of my decision, He has his orders", Shireen smiled and shook her head, replied "So why are we going into town?", Emma Greene glanced at Shireen then replied "Your uncle is going to receive his orders in person", Shireen knew with her mother was on a mission and laughed , Emma Greene finally drove away from the Greene household, turned up the radio, both Shireen and her mum put their sunglasses on, waved to all the neighbours as they drove down the street, some responded and waved with a smile, others looked in disgrace with the fact loud music was being played.

Shireen and her mum had a sing along to their favourite songs pulled up at traffic lights to go straight on, a police car pulled alongside indicating that their wanted to turn right, the two police officers looked at Shireen and her mum, Emma Greene noticed the two policemen, so waved at them, not wanted to feel left out Shireen indulged as well, the two policemen looked at each other burst out laughing and waved back, then the lights changed, Emma Greene was across that junction like a formula one driver while the police car turned right, Emma Greene turned the radio down then said "I phoned Sally and she is going to be meeting us",

Shireen knew that Marcus Greene could and would not be able to wriggle out of his birthday celebration once double trouble started, Emma and Sally Greene knew once they had their claws into Marcus Greene he couldn't win.

Before the Greene females reached the town centre Shireen started having messages off Clara and Sophie her best friends where was she , giving the usual excuses of having a revision day at home and speak in a bit seemed to quell her friends inquisitive questioning, Emma Greene turned into the long stay car park there to greet Emma and Shireen was Sally Greene, Emma Greene parked her car alongside Sally Greene's car, both Emma and Shireen exited their car had the usual hugs and kisses then made their way to see Marcus Greene, looking in the various stores along the way they came along Marcus Greene's shop, Sally Greene entered the shop closely followed by Shireen and Emma Greene they all looked in amazement at the vastness and variety of the shop, Andrea served her final customer waved to everyone and called them over then said "Well ladies, what do we owe the pleasure?", Emma Greene said to Andrea, "We've come to see you and Marcus", Andrea looked at Emma Greene in a strange way and replied "see me about what?", Emma Greene told Andrea about the surprise meal for Marcus Greene for his birthday and she was invited, Andrea was well up for a night out from her normal mid-week routine, being five foot seven tall, average figure, auburn shoulder length hair, a very attractive woman, Sally Greene said "Where's Marcus?", Andrea replied "Ladies I will give him a call", Andrea picked up the phone, dialled any said "Marcus you have three gorgeous ladies to see you".

No sooner had Andrea put the phone down there was a sound of footsteps on the floorboards of the stairs, those steps grew louder as Marcus Greene neared the ground floor, looking immaculate as usual Marcus Greene stepped of the last step, with a cheeky smile said "Ah, ladies what do I owe the pleasure?", Sally Greene decided to take charge and said "Marcus Greene, no excuses, it's your birthday tomorrow, be ready for 6:30pm prompt you will be picked up", Marcus

Greene knew he had been out manoeuvred gave a surrendering smouldering smile and said "I'm all yours ladies", Andrea, Marcus's assistant just gave a continuous grin of amusement and looked at Marcus Greene with a look of you have been caught, a general conversation broke out amongst them all, after the kisses and farewells the Greene females exited the store and made their way to the coffee shop a few doors down from Marcus Greene's emporium, Marcus Greene looked at his assistant Andrea with a bemused look on his face and said "I didn't expect that", Andrea looked at Marcus Greene burst out laughing replied "That's women power get used to it", Marcus Greene just winked and smiled at his assistant then said" I'm going back to my accounts give me a call if you need me", with a quick turn Marcus Greene disappeared up the stairs to his office.

The females of the Greene clan took the their seats, as they waited for their order of coffee and cakes, a plan of action was starting to be hatched and formulated, when bits of paper had been written on Shireen said "Can I bring some company?", Emma Greene looked at Sally Greene a quick discussion with Shireen and it was agreed that Clara her best friend could join them, Emma Greene said to Shireen "Seeing there will be a toast for Marcus's birthday, I will phone Clara's mum to see if it's ok for Clara to have a glass of wine", Emma Greene knew each other through school sports and gossiping at the school gates, Emma Greene stepped outside to make the call, Shireen and Sally Greene discussed what presents had been bought, then came the subject of who was wearing what, then bell of the coffee shop rang out then Emma Greene entered the coffee shop with Andrea following in close proximity Marcus Greene's assistant, before anyone of the Greene entourage could ask anything questions Andrea said "Marcus has sent me on a mission to retrieve two coffee's and sandwiches, he is also closing the shop early", the Greene's who had sat in formation talking to Andrea they looked gob smacked at hearing this news, as Shireen went to ask a question she was denied by the assistant who called Andrea to collect her order.

After coffee and cakes the ladies of the Greene clan packed up their various items and left the coffee shop and perused the different shops, after an hour or so Shireen spotted her uncle Marcus talking to the owner of the martial arts shop who also instructed at a martial arts club.

It was like as if both these men and Marcus Greene had a sixth sense as they knew Shireen was peering at them over a chest height billboard, both men turned and smiled and waved towards Shireen's direction, Shireen dumbfounded, stunned however you want to describe it, just smiled and waved back, Shireen quickly caught her mum and aunty up at the next shoe store still the question remained how these two mortal men could have such special senses.

After what seems like an eternal search for this, that and the other Shireen wanted to go to the local book shop, arranging to meet her mother and aunty at the car park Shireen came across the martial arts shop as it crossed her path on the way to the book shop, stopping and started glaring at the cardboard cut-out that led to the vision and feeling of ecstasy of flying on a creature that basic words could not describe, Shireen's curiosity excited her and a wanting feeling to know more about this individual who seemed to possess powers of all round perception, which led to her thoughts on her uncle Marcus, could her uncle be blessed with such unknown powers or was Shireen just clutching at straws, looking for answers to a never ending succession of visions that played out in a frustrating visions.

Shireen gathered up her thoughts, plucked the courage and entered the martial arts shop and the entrance bell rang out around the store, inside the store there was one male admiring they vast range of swords, stood at the counter two girls around Shireen's age asking about the martial arts club, a smartly dressed individual who could easily be a twin for her uncle was the instructor, the owner of this store appeared to be an easy individual to communicate with as he spoke with the two teenagers, after the bombardment of questions from the two young girls they finally booked to join the club, waiting to purchase a O Tanto sword stood a man in his early thirties, the two girls left the store, the man who waited patiently turned out to be a student of the club, this was deducted by the way the two men greeted each other.

Out of the corner of Shireen's left eye she noticed a dark haired girl, hazel eyes, about 5 foot seven inches tall, average build, roughly eighteen to nineteen years old, blue knee length skirt, white shirt sleeve blouse, light navy blue rain jacket, looking at mythical daggers, no sooner Shireen focussed her eyes back on the various swords of interest, she felt a presence cross the back of her, Shireen felt a sweet young voice whisper in her ear "Beautiful swords, maybe you should ask if you could hold one?", Shireen turned her head, as she did this female had already opened the front door, the bell of the shop rang out, the unknown female glanced in Shireen's direction waved and smiled, then disappeared into a crowd of shoppers.

The doorbell of the store rang out as the last customer departed the store, Shireen jumped as voice from behind scared her, he said, "Can I help you?", Shireen looking all shocked replied, "I'm just looking thanks", the man looked at Shireen with a puzzled and perplexed look, then uttered the words, "Thought I'd recognised you, your Marcus's niece", Shireen just smiled and replied, "Yes I am", the store owner introduced himself, "My name is Jerome, me and your uncle go a long way back, if you need anything please ask", Shireen smiled and said, "Thank you".

Shireen looked around the store and became fixated on a pair of swords in what looked like some sort of double back sheaths, it was that immediate moment that the mist descended over Shireen's eyes once again, when the mist finally evaporated out of sight, Shireen found herself in the grounds of the Tudor looking Palace, in front of her stood three men with their backs to Shireen, the two men left to right of the man in the centre she seemed to recognise, the man in the centre, he was an unknown entity, all three men wore black capes and black leather boots.

Shireen came back to the present as quickly as she left it once again, then she glanced at her watch and realised she had five minutes to return to the car park, with a brief goodbye to Jerome, Shireen left the store and scurried to the car park, as she arrived at the car park as Emma and Sally Greene placed their shopping in their cars and started chatting, Shireen made her entrance put her shopping in the car then joined in the conversation, it came to that stage in the afternoon everyone had to depart and tend to their respective families, Jason Greene had been instructed to pick his sons up from school, Emma Greene announced to Shireen that a stop at the local Garden centre would be imminent.

Emma Greene informed her daughter that while she perused the martial arts shop, Emma and Sally Greene had formulated the plans of the impending birthday celebration of Marcus Greene , on the way to the garden centre Shireen had her instructions for herself and her friend Clara of do's and don'ts, arriving at Nusea garden centre Shireen like any good P.A. had written a list of things to purchase and items to look for at the garden centre, Emma Greene stopped at the trolley bay, Shireen made a quick exit from her mother's car, insert a pound coin into the trolley, then unhitched the trolley, started pushing the trolley towards the front entrance of the store meeting her mum, Shireen stopped to look at some plants on offer, stopping to pick-up a small rose plant she then descended into a swirling extremely bright mist different from anything she had experienced, the mist opened like a curtain being drawn, standing in front of her stood a young woman with her back to Shireen, half looking back in a long white solstice dress with a flower band around her head the young woman turned fully away from Shireen, the young woman seemed familiar to Shireen, looking at this young woman from head to toe, she then discovered that this young woman was walking on a bright white carpet of cloud, that was infused with flecks of lightning rolling through the clouds with sudden bursts of extreme thunder and lightning, in the distance the young woman turned and waved then the swirling mist that brought her to this destination re-appeared just as quickly to take Shireen back to her own realm.

Shireen not understanding what was truly happening to her could only wait for the pieces from her jigsaw puzzle to fall into place, only thing she knew that this vision was totally different from anything she had experienced up until now, Shireen met her mum at the entrance to the garden centre, Shireen and Emma Greene discussed the day's events as they strolled up and down the aisles of the garden centre, Shireen turned to her mother and said "Mum, do believe our lives are planned out for us sometimes ?",Emma Greene said to Shireen "That's deep", Shireen replied "I sometimes think about life", Emma Greene thought to herself my little girl is growing up, happy that her daughter was growing into an intelligent young woman but sad that she was losing her little girl, Emma Greene turned to Shireen and said "I just take one day at a time and enjoy life, I try not to think too far ahead, otherwise life will pass you by too quickly", Shireen looked at her mum and replied "I know where I inherit my deep thoughts", both mother and daughter laughed.

With a trolley of various items Shireen and Emma Greene finally arrive at the check-out, placing the items on the checkout while Emma Greene packed apart from the compost into bags, they stayed in the trolley, after paying Shireen and mum made their way out to Emma Greene's car, everything was packed away, engine of the car started and Emma Greene and Shireen set off for home with their usual 90's cd playing, enjoying their sing-a-along, entertaining other motorists at traffic lights and junctions as they travelled home.

As Shireen and Emma Greene reached home they could see Jason Greene and sons pulling into the Greene residence with Shireen and mother in close pursuit, exiting their vehicles Jason Greene kissed his wife and said "Fish and chips all-round as order madam", cutlery, plates are set in record time, drinks orders are taken as plates are filled with food, the Greene family discussed their day with the usual repertoire of comments started flying around the family kitchen table, Shireen just ate her meal taking the odd sip of her cola thinking about her confusing term of events that afternoon, revisiting the vision of the young female gliding across the carpet made of cloud in a solstice long white dress with a band of flowers wrapped around her head, the vision was on continuous replay in her sub conscious, Shireen couldn't help but feel some sort of bizarre connection with an envious feeling thrown in for good measure for this unknown beautiful female.

After all the male members of the household had disappeared and making excuses as they went on their way, Shireen gave her mum a hand to clean-up, wash-up, Shireen said to mum "Fancy a coffee", Emma Greene replied "Yes please, you must have been reading my mind", Shireen said to her mum "Would you wrap the present I bought uncle Marcus", as Shireen filled the coffee mugs with hot water from the kettle, Emma Greene said in an inquisitive voice "What did you buy your uncle?", Shireen said in a proud voice "I bought uncle Marcus a burgundy leather writing case that was on offer in the book shop" , Emma Greene pleasantly surprised in Shireen's choice of present said to Shireen "Well, go and get it so I can see it", Shireen smiled and said "Ok, ok,", running as fast as her legs would take her, Shireen ran up the stairs ,there was rustling of bags then there was a whoosh as Shireen glided on the banister down to the hallway, Shireen making a grand entrance into kitchen with her prize purchase, handed her mum her the plastic bag with the present inside, Emma Greene opened up the plastic bag and produced a superb looking burgundy leather writing case, Emma Greene said to Shireen" Do you have wrapping paper?",Shireen then produced a roll of wrapping paper from behind her back said "Will this do?", mother and daughter burst out laughing.

It had got to that point in the evening that Shireen's siblings had to clean their teeth, have a wash, then bed, after the ceremonial protests of not wanting to wash each night, the usual unconditional surrender took place, Jason Greene's heavy footsteps could be heard descending down the stairs, the kitchen door opened up and he then said "Right, I'm going to catch the second half of the football", Before Jason Greene could ask where was his coffee Shireen knew what was coming, she was just putting one tea spoon of sugar in the coffee for Jason Greene, picking up his coffee Jason Greene strolled into the front room and settled down to watch his football game, Shireen looked at the kitchen clock which said 8,30pm,turned to her mother and said "I'm off to watch T.V.in my room", Emma Greene responded "Good night Shireen", Shireen felt an obscure feeling while negotiating the stairs to her bedroom, opening up her bedroom Shireen stripped off and changed into her pyjamas, pulling the duvet back Shireen slipped into bed pulling the duvet over her then pressed the standby button on her remote control which sent Shireen's T.V. into life.

Shireen started to watch dry humour comedy, her eyelids became heavy and heavier eventually Shireen fell asleep, whilst in such a deep sleep Shireen had never felt before, she started to experience a vision that appeared in her head as a split T.V. screen, both mists evaporated in different versions of each other, looking at this unusual vision in her head what confronted Shireen was a back of a man in a black cape, black knee high leather boots to her left, to her right stood a young woman from Shireen's earlier vision dressed in a solstice dress with a floral tiara to match, both female and male half turned as if they had wanted to look at each other but they seemed oblivious of each other, Shireen couldn't believe what was occurring in this vision both male and female looked familiar to Shireen, when she came too, waking up in a cold sweat panting and breathing heavy like a marathon runner finally reaching the finishing line.

Engaging the fan near to her bed Shireen embraced the cold breeze from her fan that sent an easing cooling affect across the whole of Shireen's body, gaining her composer Shireen's memory of the different visions that had happened to her took a twisted turn adding a piece to the jigsaw that Shireen thought belonged to a different picture, the T.V. had gone to standby so Shireen re-engaged the T.V.

Thinking that she would eventually put together the parts of her mental jigsaw had taken a rather big step backwards, like an unusual Rubik's cube that no one could solve, Shireen felt exceptionally frustrated, feeling that a challenge had been set before her, feeling more than ready to accept the gauntlet that had been laid before her, feeling that the opportunity would eventually present itself to her. Shireen just had to be patient and seize the moment when it presented itself, hopefully it would be sooner rather than later she thought to herself.

After indulging in further late night T.V. Shireen felt totally drained and no distraction could prevent her from falling asleep, as Shireen gave way to her extremely heavy eyelids which only led to her to an opening of the mist curtains once again, Shireen's dream consisted of her chasing this young woman along this never-ending road of extremely white cloud, rolling flecks of brilliant white light flew through these clouds, alternating ardent bolts of thunder and lightning burst through the clouds travelling endlessly, as Shireen thinks she is just about to make contact with this young woman, when this young woman's distance just kept on increasing Shireen finally gave up the never ending marathon too nowhere, finding that the young woman Shireen had been pursuing became an ever decreasing person in the distance, once the female had finally disappeared Shireen just felt exhausted, spinning around and around finding herself coming to a complete and sudden halt, Shireen found herself in the middle of a perpetual desert with an eternal blue sky thrown in for good measure.

Shireen found herself suspended in the air looking down on herself, there was a gradual ascending of Shireen's vision until Shireen could no longer see herself in her field of version, there was a blank black moment in Shireen's vision then the alarm clock announced its self like it did every school day morning, the day of Marcus Greene's birthday had arrived, Harry and George are to be collected by their grandparents from school as they would be staying with them for the night,rubbing her eyes Shireen decided time to arise from her bed as today was going to be a long day of anticipation on how the day was going to transpire, having a quick shower Shireen then dressed and grabbed her backpack scurried down the stairs to the kitchen, opening the kitchen Shireen was greeted by her siblings just consuming the last of their breakfast, Emma Greene gave her commands to her sons to clean their teeth, the reminder to collect their school things and their grandparents would be collecting them from school.

The 8.10 exodus took place with Shireen locking the front door, Emma Greene bungling her sons into the back of her car, Shireen opened the passenger front door, sat down, placed her backpack between her legs on the floor then put her seatbelt ,banter time in the car was exceptional as Shireen's siblings became more and more excited about spending time with their grandparents, Emma Greene pulled outside her sons school, both sons hugged and kissed their mother, Shireen opened the back nearside door, Harry and George flew out of the door, Shireen closed the car door, jumped back into the front passengers seat buckled up seat belt, turning to her mother Shireen said "So tell me what's the plan of action?", Emma Greene informed Shireen that her father would be picking up uncle Marcus and Andrea, uncle Jake and aunt Sally would make their own way to the restaurant, Shireen piped up and said "Of course Clara is coming home with us later", Emma Greene replied "Well, that's the plan of action", just smiling at Shireen, Emma Greene said "You better ask Sophie as well, you can't ask one without the other, in fact I've already spoken to Sophie's mum", Shireen looked at her mum with an embarrassed look and said "I did want to invite her but thought it would be asking too much", looking at Shireen, Emma Greene gave her daughter a reassuring smile, Emma Greene said "It's all sorted see the three of you later", with a turn of the steering wheel and indication to pull in, they had arrived at the school.

Waiting at the school best friends Clara and Sophie full of smiles, opening the door and un-doing her seat belt, Shireen got out the car both friends, Emma Greene opened her car door, left her seat, both Clara and Sophie hugged Emma Greene both said "Thanks for the invite", Emma Greene waved to Clara and Sophie's mum, they called Emma Greene over for their morning chat while the girls vanished into the school, finding themselves back in the library, Shireen and friends discussed who was wearing what make-up and all that was necessary for going out to a restaurant, Clara needed to use the bathroom, Sophie decided to retrieve drinks and snacks for everyone leaving Shireen on her own, no sooner her friends had left the swirling mist descended over Shireen's eyes wondering what dimension would enter this time, as she tried to gaze pass the mist that was taking far too long for her liking, when the swirling mist finally disappeared Shireen found herself hanging in the deep blue sky, with the wind blowing through her hair and around her body keeping Shireen suspended in a lifeless motion, she then glanced down at a gathering on the carpet of cloud with flecks of vehement white light trickling through the blanket of cloud, bursts of fervent bolts of intense thunder and lightning travelling in a never ending forward direction, all individuals lined up in formation, with three other individuals lined up facing the group all dressed in brilliant white hooded long capes.

Stretching and the extending of hands and arms, un-audible chanting the group engaged in, Shireen tried to engage the group mentally and physically to no avail, Shireen in a blink of an eye found the wind that kept her motionless intensified pulling her in an upward direction, just as Shireen's vision became obscure of the group she just had witnessed at some sort of event, Shireen found herself back in the library started to stroke her hair trying to fathom the reasoning behind her vision.

Clara and Sophie returned at the same time both holding snacks and drinks, sitting down, having a munch and sipping at a cola resumed their question and answer session the day roared by like a F1 racing car, fifteen minutes past three the girls brushed their books along the table into their backpacks, the girls fled through the doors of the library, quick pace along the corridor to the main entrance Emma Greene was waiting in her car with the engine waiting to accelerate away from the school, Shireen had pre-warned her mother she was on the way, all three girls scrambled into her mothers car ,like a getaway driver, Emma Greene sped away turning up the music as they fled into the distance, arriving at the Greene household pulling into the drive everyone clambered out of Emma Greene's car, Shireen could see that her father's minibus parked in the drive so no need to unlock the front door, opening the front door Shireen said to her two friends "Follow me", like a platoon commander leader leading her subordinates into battle, reaching the top of the stairs tried the bathroom door there was a loud deep voice Shireen knew ever so well bellowed out "Shireen I'm in here", Shireen and friends just giggled, Shireen said to her friends "Right change of plans girls, into my room", leading her friends into her room Shireen and friends they unpacked their attire for the evenings forth coming events, there was a knock on Shireen's door then the voice of Jason Greene flowed through the "Bathroom is now vacant, message from your mother, tea and crumpets ready in five mins", aloud "Yeah", came from Shireen's room ,Jason Greene laughed to himself entering his bedroom and closing the door.

Shireen taking control like a platoon commander once again issued her orders of follow me, opening the kitchen door Emma Greene said "That's good timing", as Emma Greene poured the tea with a large plate of crumpets laid before Shireen and friends, the usual girlie chat took place between Emma Greene and the girls, coming through the kitchen door all spruced up in jeans, short sleeve shirt smelling like a perfume store, Emma Greene chortled "If we lose you we can just sniff you out", Jason Greene gave his wife a glaring smile and replied "Ha, ha, very funny" ,Shireen and friends burst into raging laughter finally controlling their laughter carried on with their tea and crumpets, Jason Greene pulled up his chair next to his wife, appropriate plans formulated for later on in the evening was set in stone, the fact that plans had been changed to everyone would be travelling together made no real difference.

Jason Greene looked up at the kitchen clock on the wall which told him 5.30pm said "Time to saddle up my pony and ride off into the sunset", Emma Greene just laughed replied with a tongue in cheek comment "Young gun is off again", the females of the household burst out in profuse laughter, Jason Greene grabbed his keys off the kitchen table and gave his best I'm the man strut, closing the door behind him, the panic was on, running back and forth the bathroom ensued, the usual questions of "Does this look ok?"happened on a regular repetitive way that everyone enjoyed especially when it obtained the answer, "That looks superb", time passed so quickly that as all the females in the Greene household finally finished preparing themselves with the music bouncing off the walls, there was an opening of the front door entered Jason, Marcus, Sally Greene, followed closely by Andrea, Marcus Greene's assistant, adults had their alcohol drinks supplied, Sally Greene turned to Emma Greene winked then said in a cunning voice "What about these three young ladies?",Emma Greene looked at Sally Greene then said "What do you think?", all three girls looked at Sally Greene with anticipation replied "Well I suppose one glass won't harm", Shireen and friends had smiles like sun beams, three extra glasses of white wine was added to the list of drinks being consumed, feeling like they had finally reached the adult world, feeling like adults interjected into the conversation being discussed, finishing their drinks seemed good timing the noise of the minibus ordered blasted it's horn to announce its arrival.

Everyone climbed aboard the minibus, Shireen found herself sat next to her uncle Marcus, wearing a short sleeve summer dress sporting her bracelets on her wrists, which dazzled everyone whenever bright sunlight laid it's beams on the bracelets, making Shireen's friends Clara and Sophie envious in a nice sort of way, after a ten minute journey the minibus arrived at Something Nice Indian Restaurant, entering the restaurant Khalid the owner gave a very warm welcome, knowing the occasion Khalid informed everyone that the first drinks was on the house, Khalid knew that the Greene family are one of his best customers and a round of drinks was a good gesture on the part of the restaurant, which ended up with three large bottles of Indian lager for Marcus Greene and his brothers and two bottles of house wine for the ladies of the group, everyone produced their cards and presents ,there was handshakes, hugs and kisses as cards and presents was given in homage to Marcus Greene, only leaving Shireen to present her gift and card to Marcus Greene, Shireen stood up walked around to Marcus Greene, Marcus Greene stood up handing her present to her uncle Marcus said with a smile"Happy birthday uncle", Marcus Greene gazed into Shireen's eyes and said "Thanks Shireen", kissing Shireen on the forehead, Marcus Greene opened his present from Shireen revealing the burgundy writing case, Marcus Greene remained standing, gave a little tap on his bottle of Indian beer then said "Just a few words to say thank you for my cards and presents", as Marcus Greene took his seat Jake Greene stood up and said "Happy birthday Marcus", everyone stood up raised their glasses and bottles and said "Happy Birthday Marcus", everyone sat down, the night flew with bursts of eating and chatting, Marcus Greene turned to Shireen and said, "Thanks for the writing case, it's a lovely colour".

Shireen feeling pleased her choice of gift she had purchased for her uncle said "What's your plans for the bank holiday weekend uncle?", Marcus Greene went onto say to Shireen that Andrea was away the weekend and he would be spending the weekend altering and doing a bit of decorating to the shop, Shireen thought to herself that it would be a prime opportunity to spend some quality time with her uncle,opening her mouth formed the words "Uncle Marcus would you like me to help you the weekend?",Marcus Greene looked directly into Shireen's then said "Yes that would be a good idea, Shireen,you do need to ask your mum and dad first", turning and trying to catch her mother's attention, finally losing all patience called to her mum to no avail, it came to that time of the evening everyone had consumed and drunk enough, before Marcus Greene could take control and pay the bill Jason and Jake Greene strolled up to the bar, had a quick chat with Khalid, paid the bill, by the time everyone gathered what belongings they had brought with them the minibus driver made an entrance to inform everyone he had arrived and waiting, boarding the minibus Shireen chatted with her friends, all the adults talked about various subjects, it had got to that stage of the journey where it was just Shireen and her family and Marcus Greene left on the minibus, Shireen seized the moment and said "Mum, Dad can I stay with uncle Marcus to help him in his store this weekend ?", Emma and Jason Greene looked at each other than replied with "As long as it's ok with your uncle. it's good with me", said Jason Greene, Jason Greene looked at Emma Greene shrugged her shoulders and replied "I'm good with it", Shireen said"I will phone uncle Marcus", Emma Greene said "Can't it wait until tomorrow?", Shireen replied "Nope" Emma Greene just laughed, Shireen eased her mobile phone from her handbag, tapped into her contacts section found her uncle's name then pressed dial, it rang and rang then there a slight pause then Shireen heard her uncle's voice "Hello", Shireen was quick to reply "Hi uncle Marcus mum and dad said it's ok for the weekend", Shireen felt a tapping on her lap, looking at Shireen was Emma Greene beckoning for Shireen's phone, handing over her phone Shireen gave it grudgingly Emma Greene said "Hello Marcus are sure about having Shireen to help you the weekend?",a quick conversation ensued with Emma Greene saying "Goodbye Marcus", Emma Greene handed Shireen her mobile phone back, then said "Right, uncle Marcus has said you can stop with him the weekend, that's to help me out with the travelling". Jason Greene chipped in with" Best be behaviour", Shireen gave her father a disdainful look then uttered the words" Of course I will".

Wednesday night passed without incident apart a very deep

sleep, the next few days flew quicker than a jet fighter, Friday teatime had arrived flying through the front door like a banshee, then travelling like a bullet train up to her room, Shireen stripped of her school uniform slipping on a jogging top and bottoms then made her way down to the kitchen, Shireen realised no brothers saying to her mum "Where's my delightful brothers?",Emma Greene said "Well, seeing you are going to spend the weekend with your uncle Marcus, I've packed your brothers off to your grandparents", then added "A chance for a weekend of peace and quiet for me and your father".

Shireen looked at her mobile which showed the time of 9.30pm, deciding aimless T.V. had exhausted her interest, saying goodnight to her parents Shireen took herself up to her bedroom where she changed into her pj's, Shireen pressed the ON button of her remote control on her T.V. Shireen decided to watch some catch-up T.V. drifting off to sleep Shireen found herself with her arms fully extended out from side to side, with the rush of the wind flowing through her hair and over her body, departing the clouds Shireen was heading for the gathering she had left in a previous vision, feeling a heavy wind on the back of her legs forcing Shireen's body to manoeuvre into an upright position, landing on her feet in the centre aisle, looking down at the clouds Shireen's fascination with the flecks of bright light flickering travelling endlessly through the blanket of cloud, followed by bursts of sporadic bolts of lightning and thunder, focusing her attention forward Shireen found herself flanked from left to right by people or beings in hooded white capes, stood in front of Shireen a figure from an earlier vision dressed all in black ninja type uniform stood with their back to Shireen, standing opposite this vision in black stood the woman in the solstice dress with a flowered crown, the two seemed familiar to her ,not being close enough to see their faces, in front of these two individuals stood three beings with the hoods pulled over their heads obscuring their faces, without warning the woman in the solstice dress gently took the hand of the person in the ninja black uniform with two samurai type swords placed in a double scabbard on the back this person, Shireen looked with intense anticipation when both these beings started to turn towards each other, attempting to place her right foot forward to move closer, Shireen was thrust into the air with a sudden gust of intense wind, hanging like a kite in the air on an winters windy day Shireen could only make out the two individuals move towards each other, not being totally sure if a kiss had taken place, which infuriated Shireen immensely, as easily as the vision appeared it also disappeared the same manner.

CHAPTER FOUR
PREPERATION TIME

Shireen's alarm announced that it was 7.30am and it was time for her to exit her bed, up Shireen jumped from her bed, showered and ready for what the day will throw at Shireen, she still tried to navigate the vision in her head that haunted her in the night, throwing a few items into an overnight bag Shireen made her way down the stairs to the hallway, dumping her bag in the hallway then opening the kitchen door Emma and Jason Greene sat at the kitchen table, both with sheepish grins on their faces, Emma Greene and Jason Greene said "Morning", Shireen replied back "Morning", Emma Greene then said "Your uncle is picking you up, I dare say he will treat you to breakfast so I've just done poached eggs on toast", Shireen replied "That's fine, thanks", Jason Greene chirped in by saying "There's some money for you, knowing your uncle you won't have to pay for anything", handing Shireen an envelope, Jason Greene further said "Here is a bottle of malt whisky that your uncle enjoys, with a few cigars, I know he likes to have a puff now and again", Jason Greene then produced a plastic bag with these items inside.

No sooner Shireen had finished her breakfast there was a knock on the front door, Jason Greene opened the front door there was the greeting of "Hello bro", the kitchen door opened up, Jason and Marcus Greene entered the kitchen, greetings of hello took place around the kitchen table, Jason and Marcus Greene sat either side of the kitchen table Shireen presented the plastic bag containing the whisky and cigars then said "These are for you uncle to say thank you for this weekend", knowing that his brother had bought the items Marcus Greene looked inside the plastic bag, Marcus Greene looked up and said "Thank you Shireen, I will certainly enjoy these", Marcus Greene winked at his brother and sister-in-law and smiled, glancing at the kitchen clock Marcus Greene said to Shireen "Time to go", standing up giving hugs and kisses Marcus Greene opened the kitchen door with Shireen in pursuit, nearing the front door Marcus Greene noticed an overnight bag and said "Is this bag yours Shireen", in reply Shireen said "Yes uncle", picking Shireen's bag up Marcus Greene opened the front door, pressing the central locking button on his key fob brought Marcus Greene's brought his car to life, turning and waving to her parents at the end of the drive, Shireen's parents waved back, with a parting Shireen said "You don't need to get room with us all gone for the weekend", laughing at her parents Shireen opened the passenger door of her uncle's car sat down then closed the door, Marcus Greene hearing Shireen's comment as he closed the back door of his car said with a grin on his face, the window of the car was slightly, Shireen added to comments by saying "Be good and if you can't be good be careful", Jason and Emma Greene stood at the front door blushing and smirking like a pair of school kids.

Pulling away from his brother's house Marcus Greene said to Shireen "How was your week?", Shireen answered "Been ok studying for my exams, just chilling out with my friends, that sort of thing", on the way to her uncle's store Shireen talked about various subjects with her uncle including Wednesdays nights meal that everyone enjoyed, arriving at the back of the shop Marcus Greene turned to Shireen then said "Breakfast time", Shireen nodded in agreeance, Marcus and Shireen made the short walk from the shop to the cafe a couple of doors down from Marcus Greene's shop, entering the cafe Shireen made straight for the window table, Marcus Greene went give their order, walking the other side of the road a familiar face turned and looked directly at Shireen, feeling the presence of someone watching her Shireen looked directly across the road, Shireen recognised this young woman, by this time it had fallen into place for her, knowing where she had seen this female previously, it was at the martial arts, Shireen had a deep strong feeling within herself that this young female had some sort mystique connection to her dual jigsaw, before Shireen had time to think anything else they had arrived at Kevin's cafe, entering the cafe they found a window table, Marcus and Shireen sat down at a window table, Marcus and Shireen had one of their deep conversations about the world and it's never ending problems, orders were taken by the waitress, Shireen carried on by talking about her aim in life to become a vet or engineer, two breakfasts are delivered to their table with a pot of tea for two, both Shireen and Marcus tucked into their breakfasts enjoying every mouthful their plates soon became empty, one thing Shireen had in common with uncle, they both took great pleasure mopping up the egg yolk and other juices left on the plate with their toast.

Finishing off their tea Marcus got up and left the table to pay the bill with Shireen right behind him, Shireen opened up the door of the cafe for uncle, leaving the cafe it took five minutes to arrive back at Marcus's store ,opening up the shop Marcus Greene picked up his mail, flicking the light switch which sent the shop lights into action, Marcus Greene explained to Shireen that they would be open until midday, Shireen was all excited as it was the first time that her uncle would allow her to serve in his shop, Marcus Greene explained to Shireen how the till operated, Shireen looked the part of a shop assistant in a knee length skirt ,sky blue short sleeved blouse with black comfy shoes.

Marcus Greene opened up the shop, the shop was quiet for all of ten minutes as alot Marcus Green's customers left it until the weekend to visit the shop to see his new stock, fifteen minutes or so later the female that Shireen had eye contact with earlier that morning entered the shop, once again the two females made eye contact they both gave a smile as if to say hello, Shireen's attention was diverted away from the young female when customers started queuing to make their purchases, after the onslaught of customers the store eventually emptied of customers, Shireen noticed the female she felt had some sort of significance in her future still remained on the premises, the young female of interest had dressed herself in jeans and t-shirt in the colour of cerise, what Shireen hadn't noticed that Marcus Greene had also noticed the female in the shop maybe Marcus Greene had the same inclination !!!.

Shireen decided to introduce herself to this unknown character looking at ritual chains, pendants and artefacts, Shireen approached the female and said "Can I help you?", the female turned and said "I'm just looking thanks, mind you one or two things have caught my eyes, "before turning back to her perusing the female said "I saw you in the martial arts store the other day, my name is Joelle", before Shireen could introduce herself a quick vision entered her head, it was as if someone or thing had pushed a picture post card into her field of vision, the only thing Shireen could make out was a female in a bright white cloak, Shireen regained her focus very quickly and introduced herself "Hi I'm Shireen", the girls seemed to form a bond and feel comfortable in each other's company as they chatted, parting with the words "See you in the bit", Shireen made her way back to her uncle.

Marcus Greene made the comment "Made a new friend have you?", Shireen smiled at her uncle and said "I've seen her around and about", Marcus Greene informed Shireen that he would be going to the cash point and would buy some drinks and something to eat for their mid-morning break, parting with the words "See you in five", Marcus Greene closed the door behind him", which left Shireen and her new found friend Joelle alone in her uncle's shop,

no sooner her uncle had left the shop one of Shireen's visions burst into action, Shireen found herself in the centre of a violent vortex with extreme thunder and lightning all around her, finding herself in the centre of this vortex with static and wind flying through Shireen's body and hair, the intense vortex stretched her limbs and head, the stretching of Shireen's body and head made her bones crack, releasing severe pent up stress within her human skeleton it felt like ecstasy beyond believe, Shireen embraced her vision rather than fear it, wanting more of the experiences of being infused into a world of unknown and extreme explosions of power around her , with the shake of her head Shireen's vision came to an abrupt end.

Coming to her senses Shireen seen that her newfound friend was calling Shireen over to a glass counter, strolling over to the counter Shireen said," How can I help you?"Joelle replied "I like those pray beads, the ones that are bright white", Shireen opened the glass cabinet pulled out the tray of pure white pray beads, Joelle picked up two pray bead necklaces then said "I will have these two", taking the necklaces of Joelle, Shireen then placed the necklaces into a paper bag, handing back her change and bag containing the necklaces, Joelle placed her change into her purse then placed her purse into her bag, Joelle opened the paper bag that contained pray bead necklaces, pulling out one necklace said to Shireen "This is for you, I would like to think I've made a new friend today", Shireen taken back by Joelle's gesture said "Thank you", Joelle pointed to the post it block and pen and said "May I", Shireen replied "Yes by all means", Joelle wrote her mobile number down with her name "Call me for a coffee sometime", both girls nodded, Joelle gave a big beaming smile turned and headed for the door, as Joelle reached the shop door Marcus Greene opened the shop and held it open for Joelle with two coffees and a bag of Welsh cakes on a tray, Marcus Greene then said, "Do call again", Joelle turned and looked Marcus Greene straight in the eyes and said "I love the shop and I will certainly call again", there was a bit suspicious look in Marcus Greene's eyes, Joelle went on her way, Marcus Greene closed the door looking at his watch which told him it was 11am, still feeling suspicious and uneasy about the young lady he had just encountered reaching the counter where Shireen had positioned herself, Marcus Greene said to Shireen "Two coffees and a bag of Welsh cakes", which brought a smile to Shireen's face, Marcus

Greene said "Everything ok?", Shireen replied "Yes everything is good uncle", Marcus Greene turned to Shireen and said "You can call me Marcus, while you are here", Shireen felt that her entrance into the adult world had finally happened, with the formalities of not having to use the title of uncle to address Marcus.

Marcus Greene said "That young lady that just left the shop, was she ok?", Shireen went onto say how she had first met Joelle in the martial arts shop, then Joelle had bought two bright white pray bead necklaces and gave one of the necklaces to Shireen as a mark of friendship, then Shireen said "Joelle left me her number, she said if I would like go for a coffee to give her a call", Marcus Greene could not help his gut feeling, that there was more to the young lady than meets one's eyes, by the time coffee and Welsh cakes had been consumed, the big Victorian grandfather that had pride of place in Marcus Greene's shop announced it was midday and time to close, Marcus Greene turned to Shireen and said "Could you please close the front door", Shireen walked to the front turned the open sign to closed then turned the key to lock the front door.

Walking back to her uncle, Marcus Greene said to Shireen "I've printed out some inventory sheets, so we might as well do a small stock check as we move things around", replying to her uncle Shireen said, "Ok", Marcus Greene turned on the shops radio to help pass the time away, Shireen and Marcus Greene both looked up at the grandfather clock which said 1.45pm, Shireen managed to impale her finger on a splinter giving out the word "Ouch" Marcus Greene turned and said "Are you ok?", Shireen replied, "I've got a splinter in my finger", Marcus Green put down his clipboard, crossed the shop to Shireen, he held Shireen's hand, that's when Shireen went into a daze and her visions flowed like a dam that had just burst, Marcus Greene pulled the splinter out using a pair of tweezers, the feeling of the splinter being taken out brought her back to reality, Shireen started to wonder if Marcus her uncle was the catalyst that made her visions flood out like a tidal wave, was Shireen just barking up the wrong tree about her uncle, Shireen couldn't decide.

After applying anti-septic cream and a plaster to Shireen's finger there was a knocking on the shop door, Shireen and Marcus Greene looked up and saw that it was Shireen's friends Clara and Sophie, Shireen went over to the door of the shop, opening the door Shireen said "Hello girlies, what are you doing here?", Clara answered before Sophie could and said "I'm bored", then Sophie said "I'm bored", then both girls answered together "We are both bored", Marcus Greene and Shireen Just laughed, Sophie then said "We've come to give a hand", Shireen turned and looked at her uncle, Marcus Greene shrugged his shoulders and laughed then said "More the better", Marcus Greene went deep into thought, he then uttered the words "Right ladies I'm off to buy some baguettes and cold drinks, Shireen you're in charge, I will be about an hour I need to call somewhere", Shireen replied, "Ok, everything is under control", picking up his jacket Marcus Greene said "Have fun, see you in a bit ladies", Marcus Greene closed the shop door behind him while Shireen issued orders to her friends, unknowing to Shireen her uncle Marcus intended calling to see his friend and old army buddy Jerome Thomas, Marcus Greene is an old army buddy and friend of Jerome Thomas, being ten years older than Marcus Greene, Jerome took Marcus Greene under his wing, saving his life twice, being the same build in stature and a few differences in facial features both could be mistaken for brothers.

Entering Nusea martial arts shop Marcus Greene made directly for the main counter, reading a magazine, Jerome said without lifting his head said "Well, well, Marcus Greene what have I done to warrant your company?", Marcus Greene said "Hi Jerome, I need you to confirm something for me", Jerome lifting his head knew that this was serious by Marcus Greene's tone of voice, Jerome moved from behind the counter, closed and locked the shop door, turned to Marcus and said "Right, lovely boy let's see what have to entertain me", Jerome extended his arms out, palms facing upwards, Marcus Greene extended his arms out placing the palms of his hands onto Jerome's, a sudden vortex engulfed both men, explosive thunder and lightning erupted around Marcus and Jerome, Shireen's dreams exploded into both the men's minds, as this event was taking this place Shireen felt her visions being explored, both men after being dragged into the air and being spun around and around in this violent and disturbing vortex had a last vision, there was a last large explosive and violent burst of thunder and lightning, the vortex disappeared into infinity, Marcus and Jerome looked at each other then uttered the same sentence simultaneously "WHITE WITCHES".

Jerome looked at Marcus Greene, Marcus looked at Jerome, Marcus Greene said "Only one thing for it", Jerome nodded, Marcus pulled his mobile phone from his pocket, there was a couple of moments of ringing before there was an answer, someone then said "Hello", Marcus Green replied back "Xander, its Marcus, we need to talk", Marcus put his phone back into his pocket ,Marcus looked at Jerome and said "There's no need to come with me", Jerome gave a little laugh and replied "Are you going to deny me a bit of fun, wouldn't miss it for the world dear Marcus", smiling at Jerome, Marcus just slapped Jerome on the back and both men smiled.

Both men sat in Jerome's car, Marcus looked at Jerome and said "Are you sure about this?", Jerome nodded and said "Let's do this", starting his car they drove to the old rectory where an old school master of Marcus Greene's resided, Marcus Greene's old school master went by the name of Xander Blackstone, approximately sixty years old, black hair with streaks of grey running through his hair, five foot ten inches tall in height, average build , well educated, walking up to this large detached house Jerome grabbed Marcus's arm and said "I know you and Xander go back a long way, you need to be straight to the point and don't take any crap", Marcus Greene looked at Jerome and said "When it comes to Shireen I won't take any prisoners", Jerome smiled and replied "That's what like to hear", then grinned with a pretentious smile, watching in the front room peering through the net curtain Xander Blackstone prepared himself for his last minute guests.

Marcus Greene pressed the doorbell twice and waited, a figure came to the front door, the front door opened, stood before Marcus Greene and Jerome Thomas, Xander Blackstone dressed in black trousers black shoes, white shirt and sea green fleece, Xander Blackstone invited both men in to his house, turning to face the two men Xander Blackstone said "I believe this is an official visit, we need to have this discussion in official surroundings, opening up a large set of wooden doors from left to right, just past the largest grandfather clock you could imagine, the mechanism operated with a loud TICK TOCK as the pendulum swung back and forth, a blanket of electrified cloud appeared from top to bottom, Xander Blackstone entered first disappearing into this electrified cloud causing the cloud to ripple with bolts of lightning, the same happened when Marcus Greene and Jerome Thomas also entered this blanket of electrified cloud.

Appearing the other side of the cloud Xander Blackstone entering a massive study with a library of books and large ladders to reach them, his appearance had totally changed, now dressed in a black ninja outfit, black thigh high black leather boots, black cape, pulling the cape around himself, he sat down on rather large leather seat behind magnificent desk, making an entrance Marcus Greene dressed in the same style uniform appeared from the blanket of electrified cloud, in no mood for nonsense or being kept in the dark Marcus Greene stood right in front of Xander Blackstone's desk, Xander Blackstone looked at Marcus Greene and said" What can I do for you Marcus?",

Marcus Greene shook his head in disbelieve and said"Let's not play games Xander,what's going on?, don't tell you don't know what I mean", Xander Blackstone got up from his chair walked straight infront of Marcus Greene and said"Ok Marcus,I have had to meet with the white witch council, yes,it does involve your niece Shireen, unfortunately I can't tell you much more than that at the moment", Marcus Greene looked at Xander Blackstone with determination and eyes that could kill and said, "I hope you and White Witch council aren't playing with my niece's life", then there was a loud shutting of a book,without looking around Xander Blackstone said, "Master Jerome ,nice of you to join us", Jerome replied, "I think so".

Walking in front of Xander Blackstone dressed in the same style uniform as everyone said "Look at this, a book on white witchcraft, there's a surprise", producing a smirk on his Jerome walked straight into Xander's face and said "I don't know what games you and the White Witch Council are playing, one thing I can guarantee you, I will look for answers if anything happens to Shireen", Xander stared into Jerome's eyes and said "I know you stand in good stead with both lower and upper council, never forget I chair the lower council", Jerome just smirked in Xander's face and said "I don't care if you chair the driver's seat on the number 64 bus, I promise you this you will answer to me if anything happens to Shireen", Xander replied force fully back at Jerome while Marcus Greene just stood in amazement, "Is that a promise you can keep?", Xander Blackstone sterned faced waited for a returning volley from Jerome Thomas, then it came, the return, Jerome shock his head then said "Time will tell Xander, time will tell".

Jerome disappeared into the blanket of thundering cloud, Xander Blackstone said to Marcus Greene" Marcus if I had any other choice, I would have gladly informed you of my meeting that was convened with the White Witch Council, unfortunately it is so sensitive I can't divulge anything to you right now, when I can I will", Marcus Greene looked deeply into Xander Blackstone's eyes replied "I hope I can trust your judgement Xander", Marcus Greene disappeared into thundering cloud while Xander Blackstone sat back down in his chair, placing his elbows on his desk, then entwining his fingers, he then developed a serious frown on his face, pulling the front door behind him of the Blackstone residence, Marcus Greene opened the car door of Jerome Thomas's car, both men sat down, closed their car doors, clipped their seat belts, Marcus and Jerome looked at each other and said nothing, Jerome turned to Marcus and said "Could be worse, I could still be married", both men burst out laughing, travelling back to his store with Marcus Greene, Jerome Thomas said to Marcus Greene "What next?", Marcus Greene replied to his friend Jerome "Only one thing for it", Jerome said "I thought so, when will you do it?", Marcus Greene had a determined look on his face said "First thing tomorrow morning", Jerome replied "I thought so, I'd better get ready", Marcus Greene replied "It's going a very interesting time for all of us", Jerome nodded in agreeance.

Dropping Marcus Greene of at a Deli, Marcus Greene waved to his friend Jerome as he pulled away, Marcus Greene purchased four subs, four cans of cola, paying for his purchases Marcus Greene picked his plastic bag up and made his way back to his shop, arriving at his shop it looked totally different, Shireen and friends had made a significant effort to clean and change to the shop, Marcus Greene said "Well ladies you have certainly made a marvellous effort", placing the bag on the table said "These are for you ladies", after the consumption of food and drinks everyone entered back into the spirit of revamping the shop, Shireen took the odd glance now and again in her uncle's direction, wondering if he was part of the solution to achieving answers from her merry-go-round quagmire of dreams, thinking to herself Shireen considered the fact how would she react if any of these visions actually materialised, thoughts of different ways to react to the various scenarios that could befall her, Shireen's best conclusion was to cross that bridge when it happens.

The Grandfather clock advertised 4.30pm, Marcus Greene turned to his beautiful young helpers and said "Enough for one day", Shireen, Clara and Sophie looked up at Marcus Greene, reaching behind the counter Marcus Greene clasped three envelopes in his hand, walked towards Shireen and her friends, Marcus Greene said as he handed the envelopes to the three girls "This is for you young ladies, your help has been much appreciated today a little something to say thank you", this gift of generosity put the brightest of smiles of these young ladies faces, all three girls gave a big thank you to Marcus Greene followed by a hug and a kiss on the cheek from Shireen, Clara and Sophie followed in Shireen's display of affection for Marcus Greene, Marcus Greene said "Well ladies time to get you home", Marcus Greene lived above his shop which had three levels to it with a roof garden, many a time Marcus Greene would sit in his roof garden perusing the Nusea night life, Marcus Greene turned to Shireen and said "You know where everything is Shireen for a shower or bath", Marcus Greene closed the door behind him, Shireen climbed the stairs up to the Marcus Greene lair on the third floor, the door was a heavy red oak door, opening up the apartment door, Shireen entered into the apartment, the apartment had a deep glistening red oak floor with beautiful Persian rugs placed in order around the floor, deep burgundy leather two and three seat sofas with a couple of armchairs thrown in for good measure, the main room was a large room with various doors leading off it, all around the room there was handmade bookshelves from the very bottom that crawled right to the very top of the tall ceilings, books on every subject you can imagine and existed could be found in this personal library, the main features that really gave the apartment an exclusive look was a big open fire place and a very unusual grandfather clock, the grandfather clock was a large clock with one front forward with two angled faces right and left of the centre face, large lamps on small tables scattered around the room with bright LED bulbs in them, the main lights had intriguing light shades wrapped around the bulb holder, this gave the room an unusual warmth and ambience of relaxation and extreme comfort.

Shireen saw the hand written gold sign on one of the doors that said "GUEST ROOM", staying in this room before Shireen felt very comfortable in this lavish but somehow room of contentment, opening up the door Shireen entered up the room which was full of neutral colours, a large comfortable bed with a bedside table either side with a glorious lamp on each of the tables, to the left was a door which led to an en-suite which had magnificent granite grey colour tiles on the floor and walls with a light grey ceiling, a cascade of spotlights in the ceiling and walls that ran through the bathroom that gave the impression of watching the universe whilst sat in the bath, Shireen sat in her bath of bubbles thinking that this is one her most enjoyable times she had encountered for a long time, no screaming brothers, no banging on the door and the words of "Have you finished", to contend with while relaxing in the bath.

After her bath, Shireen dressed herself in navy blue knee length culottes and a white blouse, putting on a pair of navy high heel shoes and a little make-up to round things up, making an entrance into the Marcus Greene's lair, Shireen found her uncle already spruced up ready for anything, Marcus Greene said to Shireen" I take it we are going out for an evening meal", Shireen looked at the uncle and laughed then replied "I guess so", Marcus Greene dressed impeccably as usual in a pair of navy blue trousers, beige short sleeve shirt and a black pair of air soled shoes, so highly cleaned that you could see the gleam bounce off his shoes, even when the light dared to make a slight glance at his shoes they stood out, looking for a pre-set number in his phone sat in his favourite armchair, Marcus Greene pressed the contact of Miguel's brassiere, within seconds there was a reply, Marcus Greene replied "Miguel, it's Marcus, just wondering do you have a table for two?", Shireen could hear the man on the other end of the phone say "Marcus my friend, I will always have a table for you", Marcus Greene then said "See at eight pm", Marcus Greene looked at his very unique three sided faced grandfather clock which conveyed the time of seven forty pm, there was a sudden ring of Shireen's mobile, well if you can call it that it was more like dance trance tune, answering her phone Shireen said "Hello", then came the ultimate "Mother what now", then "Yes, yes, YES," then Shireen said "Uncle Marcus, for you, my never trusting mother "Marcus Greene went off into conversation with Emma Greene, once he had finished his phone call with his sister-in-law, turned to Shireen and said "Strike a pose", ,Shireen enforcing a smile and a supermodel strut, Marcus Greene thinking he was a professional photographer finally took a picture, pressing a few items on her phone, then sent a picture to Emma Greene, Marcus Greene then said

"Your little girl is no longer, She is now a young woman", a few more words went back and forth between Marcus Greene and Emma Greene, handing back her phone to Shireen, Marcus Greene said with a sympathetic smile "Your mum", Shireen uttered the words "Yes mother ?", then came "Yes mother, ok mother, goodbye mother", then gave a growl at her phone, Marcus Greene trying to be witty said "Your mother was it ?", sticking her tongue out at Marcus Greene said "I'm starving" Marcus Greene couldn't help himself feeling he was on a witty roll replied "I'm Marcus, nice to meet you starving", Shireen replied with a sarcastic return of "Ha, ha, my sides are splitting".

Marcus and Shireen picked up their jackets made their down the two flights of stairs to the front of the shop, closing the shop door and locking the front door of the shop door behind the both of them, made their way to Miguel's Brassiere which was about a five minute walk from Marcus Greene's home, entering the restaurant Shireen and Marcus Greene had a welcome off Miguel as if they if long lost family had turned up on the doorstep rather than customers, which reiterated Shireen's believe that her uncle was a well-respected and liked man, taking their seats Marcus Greene ordered a bottle of Merlot red wine and a medium bottle of sparking soda water, as quickly as the drinks order was taken, the order arrived at the table, one chilling bottle of Merlot, ice bucket and of course a bottle of sparkling soda water ,Shireen looked in anticipation of what was about to transpire, placing ice into two highball glasses followed by Merlot wine topped up with soda water, Marcus Greene said raising his glass "Your first spritzer, to your dreams and your future, I hope they come true for you", Shireen had a little glint of a tear in her eye and replied in the same positive manner "The same to you my dear uncle Marcus", before any other words could part from their lips there was a tap on Marcus Greene's shoulder, Marcus Greene instantly said without any hesitation in his voice "Xander Blackstone",

Xander Blackstone with an intense curious stare in Shireen's direction said to Marcus Greene "Are you not going to introduce me to this lovely young lady", raising himself out of his seat turning to face Xander Blackstone, looking Xander Blackstone square into his eyes said in a stern but friendly voice "Shireen I would like you to meet Xander Blackstone, Xander Blackstone I would like you meet my niece Shireen", moving in a reluctant manner Marcus Greene moved out the way, shaking Shireen's hand Xander Blackstone said in a very intriguing voice "A pleasure to meet you my dear, I'm sure our paths will cross again sometime soon, must dash Marcus old chap, the wife and I are off to the theatre", Shireen returned the compliment and replied "A pleasure to meet you Xander", Xander Blackstone put on his jacket, headed straight back to Marcus Greene, shaking Marcus Greene's hand and said "See you soon", then turned to Shireen and said "Once again a pleasure my dear", Xander Blackstone's wife just waved and said "Hi", following Xander Blackstone out of the Brassiere.

Marcus Greene sat back in his chair, ordering for himself and Shireen seen his mobile phone vibrate in his jacket, taking his phone out of his jacket, opened up the cover on his phone, a message from Xander Blackstone with a direct and to the point sentence "An ideal candidate", after their main course they both finished with a fresh fruit salad, last of the spritzers, cheese and biscuits and floater coffee for Shireen and a Irish coffee for Marcus Greene, Miguel arrived at the Greene table to enquire about Marcus and Shireen's experience of the restaurant that evening, both gave Miguel the recognition that he so much desired about their experience at the brasserie that night was an absolute culinary delight.

Offering another round of coffee's on the house that Miguel insisted they accept, Marcus and Shireen did not offer any resistance and graciously agreed to Miguel's hospitality, taking the final sips of the second round of delectable coffee's with bursts of conversation on every topic you could imagine, Marcus and Shireen putting their lips, tilting their heads and glasses back so the last of the coffee's would trickle from the bottom of glass mugs to their lips, leaving the little river of coffee left travel pass their lips and along their tongues to the very back of their throats and disappear, Marcus Greene paid the bill by credit card and gave a generous tip then said to Shireen, "Right, my dear time for us to go", Shireen looked at Marcus Greene and said "I don't think I can move, I'm so full",

Finally making to the front door of the Brassiere, Miguel opened the front door and said with a large smile "Please both call again", Shireen and Marcus Greene shook Miguel's hand and disappeared into the night back to Marcus Greene's place of residence, Reaching the front door of his business and home, Marcus Greene opened up the front door turning the alarm off, with Shireen in close proximity made their way to the door which lead to the stairs which with effort in climbing would bring both Marcus and Shireen to the apartment upstairs, re-setting the alarm Marcus Greene closed the door to the shop, opening the front door of the apartment Shireen said to her uncle "I'm so tired, I'm off to bed, thank you for everything", after pouring himself a large malt whiskey, glass in his right hand kissed Shireen on the forehead and said "You are welcome, night, night", Shireen opened up the guest room, falling onto the bed kicking off her shoes, pulled the duvet over her, meanwhile Marcus Greene sat in his favourite armchair, opened up his phone which had been placed on a coffee table and re-read the message from Xander Blackstone, swirling his malt whisky in a clockwise motion, the ice in the glass made a clinking tune that could not be recognised, Marcus Greene started to doubt his actions involving his niece Shireen, then arrived at the conclusion that Shireen's all round personality would be wasted if she didn't reach her true potential, what awaited for Shireen would truly enhance her way to adulthood, Marcus Greene said goodnight to his empty whisky glass then retired to his bedroom, Shireen drifted into a dream of serenity, that wouldn't last as Shireen envisage herself as a small child trying to make an ill-fitting jigsaw to conform into a moving video of her previous visions, re-trying as this small child Shireen could see herself on a blanket of cloud kneeling down pounding large video moving jigsaw piece's into a non-achievable pattern.

The new day arrived as quickly as the night departed, waking-up from her deep refreshing sleep Shireen could smell breakfast being cooked, showered within minutes Shireen made her entrance in a grey tracksuit and trainers, sitting down at the breakfast bar Shireen said "Good morning", to her uncle and Marcus Greene replied the same with a brightness in his voice "Good morning Shireen, bacon and mushroom omelette ok ?", Shireen replied "That's great", with some French toast breakfast was soon consumed, devouring the last of her breakfast Shireen placed her plate by the kitchen sink, Shireen sat back down at the breakfast bar as Marcus Greene sorted through the news headlines on his laptop, Marcus Greene turning his laptop off and placing it to onside, Shireen sat back down opposite her uncle.

Marcus Greene placed Shireen's hands in his hands then the bombshell delivered itself, Marcus Greene announces that he knew of Shireen's visions because he is the one who is the one responsible for placing them in her mind, wanting to see Shireen's response to her visions what Marcus Greene didn't divulge is that he knew about the visions of the white witches, Marcus Greene needed a true indication of suitability to the circle and to the order of light and life, Shireen had an expression of being flabbergasted on her young and innocent face, Marcus Greene asked Shireen to keep her eyes closed and all would be revealed to her, Marcus Greene told Shireen through thought and sight process I will guide you from the past to the present not in this realm but a realm alien to you and this world as you know it, Marcus Greene started his journey of explaining The Beacon of life to Shireen and how She as one individual played a major part in an intricate web that was going to be revealed by her uncle.

Marcus Greene started off his tour with back in a realm older than what we know of our earth you have the realm of the land of life, this land is governed by the Beacon and the councils of life that gives life, at the palace of life the Beacon is situated in the palace grounds, there are two chambers, the upper chamber is for masters of light and life whom have travelled from mortal to immortal, their decision is final when advice is sought, the keeper of the light and life can also convey their decision to the Beacon, the Beacon will overturn any decision that it feels unjust and not in the best interest of everyone conveyed through the keeper of the Beacon, for most decisions of state the lower chamber is entrusted with this responsibility, Shireen could see everything in vivid 3D motion as her uncle continued on with his description of this realm of the unknown to Shireen.

CHAPTER FIVE
TRAINING TIME

Marcus Greene explained that what Shireen was about to encounter will not have any rhyme or reasoning in her mind, making it noticeably clear that Shireen should just accept about the forth coming events and beings that she will encounter if she should choose to become a Protector,

explaining to Shireen that the Land of life was a central hub for trade amongst other beings from other realms, ultimately from these other realms also came evil participants in search of ways to take control of the Beacon of light and life, once the these evil entities gain control of the Beacon then they would gain access to other realms and extract all they could and enslave the beings, time had a different essence as one minute of human time was one hour in the land of life time, should Shireen accept the invitation to become a Protector then a clone would be sent to cover any absence when Shireen is engaged by the circle of life, the circle of life was a unique union of beings from different realms, like modern day officer corps that would lead the army of life against their foes, one such evil empire was The Realm of The Dark Nexus, the most feared and hated by all, The Realm of The Dark Nexus had a most vile and evil Queen, a fallen white witch with an axe to grind with everyone, torture was a fun pass time for the Queen, she would watch someone being tortured like we would watch a movie, she would be extremely enthralled and excited by the thought of someone in excruciating pain, Katarina was the name of this evil and vile excuse for a Queen. Queen Katarina of The Realm of The Dark Nexus on one occasion sat and watched with intense excitement, dressed in a long black lace and satin dress with a wrap around head scarf also in lace and satin, her face was dawned with blackcurrant red eye shadow right to the very corners of her eyelids, with the same colour lipstick that caressed her lips to the very corners of her mouth, searing, hypnotic blue eyes that could snare anyone with a soul, the final touch to this horrific, sadistic, despicable , evil woman, a crown of white gold formed in the shape of large thorns entwined with each other, pulsating number of white lights in a never-ending race spiralled around the crown, Katarina left her armchair of comfort, long black polished finger nails that came to a sharp needle point had a surprise of their own, dragging her nails along her victims chest, Katarina took extreme delightful ecstasy knowing her victim was suffering immense pain, for good measure Katarina's nails released acid from the tips of needle like nails leaving deep culverts along her victims chest, as her victim convulsed in agonising pain Katarina flung her head back, her arms reached into the air and shrieked in absolute ecstasy, this is just one horrific story, some swear she had the DNA of a female praying mantis, first would come sexual gratification, then her victims being devour in some shape or fashion, if her victims escaped death then they thought themselves beyond very lucky.

Shireen's reaction was one of dis-belief, not knowing whether she was sickened by this individual or intrigued by the fact of what could turn someone into such a monster, Marcus Greened called to Shireen and asked, "Are you ok? Do you want me to continue?", Shireen just nodded yes,

Marcus Greene further informed Shireen she would have attend Cadre of life to acquire weapon and tactics knowledge, further more Marcus Greene brought up the subject of Shireen's bracelets and the power that they possess, how sexy Sandra that Shireen named was a Protector, the bracelets had belonged to Sandra and she wanted to meet Shireen before relinquishing her bracelets that had many years of power and knowledge, Shireen would have been given new bracelets by the Beacon and order but the alternative appealed to Marcus and Shireen more, this was a honour very rarely given to someone being proposed for the circle of life.

Furthermore Marcus Greene told Shireen the bracelets held great powers, from translating with other species to creating great surges of power for supplying weapons with ammunition, if you decide to become a protector then more will be revealed to you about the capabilities of your bracelets, Marcus Greene asked Shireen to open your eyes and said "The choice is yours Shireen, you have a couple of days at the most", Shireen looked at her uncle and with delight on her face said "Let's do it", Marcus Greene looked at Shireen very intensely and said "You are a hundred percent about this" ?, Marcus said to Shireen "You will need your bracelets ", Shireen went into the guests room and reappeared very quickly with her bracelets on, looking at her uncle she could see he had an identical pair of bracelets, Shireen sat down opposite her uncle, Marcus then said "Place your hands together as if you are going to pray, the bracelets will do the rest", Shireen did as she was instructed, within seconds Shireen found herself in a violent vortex spinning around and around, flecks of golden light swarming around and around through the vortex, followed by thunderous bolts of lightning shooting through the vortex and exploding, Shireen came too, finding herself in anextra-long test tube not going up, not going down, just hovering being supported by just a warm pleasant breeze with a light as bright as day above her head, then there was blast of bright light which revealed Shireen's clone directly opposite Shireen, the clone pushed her hands against the soft rubber like wall of the tube distorting the tubes shape, Shireen did exactly the same as the clone had just done, their palms of their hands making contact through this very soft like substance, the clone said through telepathy "Lovely to see you again, I told you our paths would meet again", Before Shireen could reply the clone winked flirtatious manner and everything went black and there was a massive burst of bright light.

Blinded by the blast of light heard the familiar voice of her uncle calling "Shireen, Shireen", coming too her senses

Shireen found herself at a place she had once dreamt about, THE PALACE, looking directly at her uncle dressed in a ninja type uniform, black armoured jacket with a black cape with a set of two swords strapped to his back, looking herself up and down Shireen had transformed exactly the same as her uncle in appearance, taking Shireen by the hand Marcus Greene said to Shireen "Well come to your new world", then gave Shireen a reassuring smile, looking around her surroundings Shireen was mesmerized by the sheer size of her new world, Shireen sensing a powerful force transmitting enormous energy from behind her, turning on the balls of her feet pivoting 180 degrees, nearly falling over in disbelieve stood larger than life The Beacon of Life, seeing this unbelievable site of mass and natural light show of flickering platinum flecks with bursts of blue and platinum bolts of lightning shooting from top to bottom, the bracelets on Shireen's wrist started to pulsate with glowing blue and platinum white light, turning back to her uncle, Marcus Greene said "Beautiful isn't it", no sooner had Marcus Greene made his comment Marcus Greene felt a presence he knew so well, then he felt a left hand grab his left buttock, Marcus Greene without flinching said "My dear Delores", this is a woman of breeding, 5'8"tall, average body, brunette colour, In a deep southern accent from Alabama came the reply from this elegant woman when Marcus Greene came face to face with this female named Delores, "Marcus Greene, you handsome man, when are you going to make an honest woman of me ?", Marcus Greene replied "Soon my dear Delores, soon", then smirked, Delores putting her arms around Marcus Greene's waist and said " Your such a tease Marcus Greene, one day, one day, you will give in".

Delores then said" Where are my manners, this is my niece Savannah", Savannah stepped forward and kissed Marcus Greene on the cheek, taking Marcus Greene by surprise then said "A pleasure sir", Marcus Greene replied "The pleasure is all mine", Savannah gave a glowing and seductive smile then whispered to aunty "My, my he's a handsome man", Delores nodded in agreeance, Savannah stood 5'8" tall same height as her aunty, brunette hair with a slender figure, Marcus Greene then introduced his niece Shireen to Delores and Savannah, clutching Shireen on her waste Delores said in her southern seductive voice "The good looks certainly run consistent in your family", Savannah embraced Shireen as if she was a sister and kissed her on the cheek and said "Pleased to meet you", Shireen replied with the same courtesy back "Pleased to meet you!".

Before any other pleasantries could take place there was an announcement that came from a balcony from none other than Xander Blackstone, "Would Master Marcus and Master Jerome and all other master's please pray witness",

Marcus Green turned swiftly towards Shireen and said, "Sandra is going to propose you, don't be perplexed everything will be fine, just do as you are instructed",

Marcus Greene and Jerome entered the platform, nodding in recognition to each other amongst the masters, Xander Blackstone made the announcement that echoed loud and clear around the Palace grounds, Shireen turned and was utterly surprised to see the man she had met in the restaurant now before her, "Well come all of you, you have been chosen for an adventure of a lifetime to do good and combat evil", looking at his new recruits to see who might fail and who might succeed continued with his speech "It is not going to be an easy journey, but a tremendous experience that will remain deeply in your heart and mind whilst you live", Xander Blackstone went onto say " Some of you will fail, some will succeed, all I can say is be true to yourself, that is most important thing.

Xander Blackstone barked his orders "Proposers present your Neophyte", Sandra placed her hand around Shireen's hand and said " Don't be scared, just do as you are instructed to do", then smiled and winked, Sandra and Shireen walked towards the Beacon that started to come to life, like a massive glitter ball the sphere came to life shooting beams of high intensity light around the palace, there was a line that was about six feet in circumference away from the Beacon,

Sandra and the rest of the proposers place their Neophyte on this line, The voice of Xander Blackstone spoke in a rigid and not to be questioned voice " Neophyte present your arms up in front of you with your palms of your hands facing towards the Beacon", it was as if the Beacon had grown instant arms that extended towards each Neophyte, the arms of the Beacon entwined it's self around the hands of each Neophyte, the sphere started rotating in a clockwise motion, the speed of the sphere intensified sending a pulsating light information through the beacon with a strobing effect following shortly afterwards, the penetrating beams of light off the sphere gave everyone present a lightshow that was an unforgettable experience, first slowly, faster and faster the sphere spun, Shireen felt she was in ecstasy as the lights in sequence reached her arms, followed rapidly by the strobing energy reaching Shireen's young body, sending sensations and sensitivity through her mind and body, Marcus Greene watched as his niece was no longer a little girl he once shared pretend tea parties with but a young lady and soon to be warrior.

As the intense induction ceremony reached its climax, Shireen's eye sockets and open mouth glowed with an intense sky blue, glorious white glow, as the ceremony started to wither down and retract slowly, so did the brightness of the glow that occupied Shireen's body, the array of lights and sensations finally started to fizzle out until all that remained was flecks of light cascading from top to bottom of Shireen's eyes, Shireen started to gain her faculties only to realise that Sandra had picked up the spare pair of new bracelets intended for Shireen, Sandra had went through the whole inauguration ceremony again, not knowing the reason for Sandra's decision Shireen knew that this would transpire soon enough, Sandra took Shireen's hand and looked at Shireen and said "Now the fun begins", Shireen took Sandra's hand as she did Xander Blackstone announced "Neophytes it is time for your training to begin, it is up to you to decide your fate, to succeed or fail "taking a deep look from left to right, looking at those who stood before him, Xander Blackstone said "Proposers it is with your guidance and teaching that will decide your Neophytes destiny, for now I say farewell", Xander Blackstone turned around swiftly and looked at each master with an intense glare and said "You know your orders carry them out, Marcus Greene looked intensely at his niece as she was led away by Sandra into the palace of light and life, Xander Blackstone turned in the direction of Marcus Greene and looked intensely into Marcus Greene's eyes and said "My study Master Marcus, if you would be so kind", replying with the grace as it was received Marcus Greene said "Certainly Lord Chancellor Blackstone", Marcus Greene started to follow Xander Blackstone as he walked towards his study with the masters bowing in honour of his departing presence, Jerome grabbed Marcus Greene's arm and said "If you need me, just call me", Marcus Greene smiled and said "Thank you".

With a flick of his hand Xander Blackstone opened up his heavy wooden doors to his study, with a flick of his fingers the superbly carved wooden chair slid with grace from under the magnificent carved table, Xander Blackstone sat in his chair behind his desk, flicking his fingers once more a chair slid from under the desk on the opposite side of Xander Blackstone's desk, Xander Blackstone invited Marcus Greene to take a seat, Marcus Greene sat down, crossed his legs and waited for Xander Blackstone to talk, inter-locking his fingers resting his elbows on the arms of his chair Xander Blackstone said "Marcus my dear friend, it's time for you to find out the truth", Marcus Greene replied "The truth about what ?", Xander Blackstone said" We must make a journey to the White Witch Kingdom, all will be revealed", with a clap of his hands Xander Blackstone instructed the doors of his study to close as the conversation between Lord Chancellor Xander Blackstone and Master Marcus Greene intensified.

Sandra turned to Shireen a took her hand and said" Time for some refreshments my dear", taking Shireen by the hand guided Shireen towards the main entrance of the Palace of Life, surrounded by a ring of palace guard that swore allegiance to defend or die to protect all, entering a massive hallway, the walls supported portraits of people and beings nobody that Shireen recognised, Sandra then gave an in-depth accountant of the portraits and the people and beings in them, informing Shireen that all had the honour of passing onto the upper chamber, in the Great hall portraits of lower chamber where she recognised her uncle as one of the masters and a member of the lower chamber council.

In the Great Hall Shireen took refreshments with all the other Proposers and Neophytes, Shireen looked around in utter amazement at the various beings and creatures that surrounded Shireen and Sandra, As Shireen consumed the last of her refreshments Sandra said "Time for me start your training and show you your quarters", taking hold of Shireen's hands Sandra then said Shireen "Your training is going to be unconventional, nothing like you have ever experienced before, just let your mind and body flow like water finding its way down river", walking into a hallway that looked as if was never ending, each Proposer and Neophyte disappeared into a room that had their name on the door, in whatever was their language they understood, feeling like she had walked endless miles on a fruitless journey, finally arrived at a door on her left, with Shireen's name and Sandra's name had been placed on the door of her room, Shireen stood facing the door in complete disbelief on her journey so far, opening up the door to her room was an incredible experience from what she thought the room was going to be beyond Shireen's wildest expectations, Shireen entered the room as if she was entering an Arabian tent.

Sandra sat down on a pile of very large comfortable scatter cushions Sandra then said "Shireen please sit down opposite me", looking into Shireen's eyes Sandra said "Don't be scared, you are about to endure practices and procedures uncommon to you", Sandra placed arms and open hands, palms facing upwards on a pile of cushions, Sandra then said "Shireen I want you to hold onto my wrists", Shireen did as requested by Sandra, Sandra then held Shireen's wrists, the bracelets of both Shireen and Sandra started to glow an intense bright blue and white colour, a vortex appeared from nowhere engulfing Shireen and Sandra, the vortex with persistent intensity, flecks of light filtering like rain drops through the vortex, with an odd crack of thunderbolt penetrating its way through the vortex.

With a flash and a bang Shireen and Sandra found themselves in an old style gymnasium, Still sat down holding each other's wrists, Sandra said "Might be an idea to stand up", chuckling as she said it, Shireen replied "Yep, I think so, Shireen looking around her new surroundings said "This is impressive", Sandra said "I think so", Shireen looked around her new surrounds on a 360 degree pivot, overawed by the different types of weapons on displayed, not knowing if she stood in a 3D dream or in reality, Shireen decided just to go with the flow, steadying herself Shireen from behind by her shoulders Sandra said" In this place of greatness and learning and mentoring, you learn to defend yourself with weapons, with your hands, with your mind", turning to face Shireen and placing her hands on her shoulders further said "You must move without tension in your body, flow like the wind and strike like a torrent river",

Sandra picked up two Jo Staffs from a rack then, placing one in Shireen's hands said "Let's see what you have got girlie", striking from left to right at Shireen's torso, Shireen blocked then counter attacked, like ballet both females spun around attacking each other, Sandra out manoeuvring Shireen then flipped Shireen's legs with one strike from her Jo Staff, pulling up Shireen by her hand, Sandra said "Very good, let's try that again", so both Shireen and Sandra did it again, again and again until Sandra considered Shireen competent enough to say "Ok, time to try something else", placing the Jo Staff's back in the rack then picking up two Bokken wooden swords, Sandra turned to Shireen smiling and said "Let's see what you can do with this ?", Squaring up to each other Sandra winked then struck out at Shireen's throat, Shireen blocked and counter attacked, Sandra spun around out of the attack, this went on and on until Sandra said "That's enough for one day, bowing to each other Sandra kneeled down followed by Shireen, placing their arms together their bracelets started to glow once again, A vortex initiated before the two females knew what had happened to them the vortex was in full swing, flash, bang and wallop, as quick as the vortex started it came to an abrupt end, finding themselves back in there accommodation.

Finding themselves in the position they originally started from with both Sandra and Shireen holding arms, Sandra said "That was fun", Shireen said to Sandra "What next?", Sandra told Shireen that food and refreshments would be delivered to their room, Sandra lifted her right pointing to a door said "That is the bathroom, the door next to it is your bedroom", Shireen said to Sandra "Where are you going to sleep ?", Sandra smiled and said "I'll be fine here plenty of cushions", both Shireen and Sandra laughed, there was a sudden knock on the door that startled both Shireen and Sandra, Sandra called out "Who is there ?", there was a deep loud voice that replied "The officer of the palace guard", looking weary at the door, reaching inside her body armour Sandra opened the door to the room reaching inside her body armour, stood at the door was a large individual, with a head covering protection so this individuals face was obscured , pulling the door partially behind her, Sandra, indulging in conversation, Shireen could only hear snippets of the conversation, what she heard was of interest, sentences of interest that made Shireen take notice, "Guards are outside your door, outside the window and in the entrance to this hallway", Shireen knew if she asked questions she would be fobbed of with petty excuses of reassurances that would frustrate her, Shireen thought it would be in her interests to observe and wait for the right opportunity , Sandra wheeled in a trolley of food and refreshments, as Shireen and Sandra sat down for their meal there was a knock on the door, Sandra said in a mutter "what now, "the same performance took place "WHO's there?", the reply that came back surprised Sandra "It's Delores", opening up the door with her right hand in her body armour, stood directly in the doorway was Delores and Savannah, Delores one hand on hip, one hand the doorway reaching in an upwards manner "hiya ladies, need some company", Savannah went to sit with Shireen, Delores said to Sandra "A quick word if I may", to Sandra, out of ear shot of Shireen and Savannah Delores said "Marcus has told me there is going to be a kidnap attempt on Shireen, the lord chancellor has ordered me train with you and Shireen, not forgetting Savannah", Delores continued by saying that Shireen is a highly valued prize by the Realm of the Dark Nexus and all efforts should be made to protect her, putting a smile on their faces entered back into the room Delores said "I don't know about you ladies I'm hungry", everyone nodded in agreeance and started to eat what was on a very large serving trolley.

It arrived at that time of night where everyone felt tired, apart from Sandra and Delores, they just played along as they knew and felt an imminent danger and a sense of evil in the air, Sandra and Delores knew that with these strong senses and feelings of danger grasping at their very souls a tight guard had to be maintained, it was agreed that Shireen and Savannah should share the bed while Sandra and Delores would make do with the huge pile of comfortable cushions, Shireen and Savannah did not protest or ask questions as they're bodies ached, tired and with soreness from the day's events any form of protest was not available from both girls, Sandra and Delores formulated a plan of guarding the room, Delores started to nod through tiredness when there was a commotion outside the door and trying of the door handle, Sandra jumped up, both women drew their swords which glowed in a blue and white brightness, Sandra looked out the window to see guards in combat with darkly dressed figures then there was a shout "CALL OUT THE PALACE GUARD ", within seconds the Palace alarm sounded, the guard dogs had be unleashed, a large wolf hound that no entity would want to come into contact with these ferocious beasts, as these fantastic creatures neared the black shadows disappeared into the night, there was a banging of the door which woke-up Shireen and Savannah,

A large heavy sounding voice called out "Madame, it's the

Palace guard", stood before Delores was the captain of the guard, he stood at least six foot six inches tall, dressed in a dark menacing uniform with a black reflective face covering, "Are you okay Madame", she replied "I'm all the better for seeing you and your guards", and smiled, "Delores said "Was any of the guards injured ", the guard captain replied "Thank you for your concern, a few stitches will be needed and a few bruises tendered too, we will survive", nodding his head turned and walked away, making sure that extra guards had been placed outside the door and placed extra guards outside the window of the women inside.

It was roughly 5pm when Shireen's mobile phone rang out across Marcus Greene's flat, Shireen's clone looked at Marcus Greene's clone, Marcus Greene's clone said to Shireen's clone "You had better answer that", looking to see who the caller was Shireen's clone saw the word mum flash upon the screen of the phone, pressing the answer icon on the phone said "HI mum", the voice on the other end said "Hi Shireen, everything ok?", Shireen's clone answered "Yes mum, everything is fine", a back and forth conversation took place between Shireen's clone and Emma Greene, finally Emma Greene said can I speak to your uncle, taking the phone from her ear, made the meaning to Marcus Greene's clone that he was required to speak to the person on the phone, Shireen's clone then said handing over "Uncle Marcus, mum would like a word",

Marcus Greene's clone took the phone and placed it to his ear and said "Hi Emma, how are you?", Emma Greene replied "Hi Marcus, I'm good thanks, is Shireen behaving herself ?", the clone replied "Yes, like an angel", Emma Greene then said "Seeing it's a bank holiday we are going to have a barbecue tomorrow, no need to worry about transport it's all arranged, no excuses not to turn up", the clone replied "Ok, we will be waiting", Emma Greene then said "Pick you up at 2:30pm",the clone replied "Ok, see you then", pressing the end call icon the clone looked at the other clone, then said "This message must be passed on", clasping each other's arms just above their hands closed their eyes, then there was a glowing orb around them as they transmitted their message by some sort of advanced telepathy.

Queen Katarina who ruled The Realm of the Dark Nexus with an iron fist, called for her chief aid, as he entered Queen Katarina's court, he bowed, Queen Katarina stood with supreme air of superior grace with an evil chilling presence around her demeanour, dressed in a deep black flowing dress, with her thorn like crown that flowed with flecks intense light and electricity around her crown, pale face and blood red lips said "What news do you have for me?", the aid so scared said "My Queen, The Palace of Life is heavily protected and secure, if we are to achieve capturing our goal we must lure it away from the Palace Life", knowing that this was the truth about the palace Life said "You have two passing's of the moon to formulate a plan, fail me this time and you will beg me to end your life", the aid replied "Yes my queen", then scurried out of the court, turning to her family said" The time nears to achieve our goal, make sure everything else is in place" then retreated to her own private quarters followed closely by her ladies in waiting and guards.

Early morning had arrived, there was a large bang on the door, then a voice said, "Morning food my lady", opening the door a trolley of food was to greet the eyes of Sandra, also outside was a heavy guard presence of rather tall stocky built guards, all in black body armour with face protectors and heavily armed with what resembles a Japanese Naginata long handled weapon and a samurai looking machete sword.

Sandra said thank you to the guards officer, pushed the large trolley inside, everyone took fresh clothing that was in a large cupboard then put on their body armour on, consumed their morning meal, it was at that point that Savannah said "Can we train together today", Delores chipped in and said "That's a good idea", Sandra shrugged her shoulders and said "I'm ok with it, how about you Shireen?", smiling she said "It's good with me", As they made themselves comfortable by kneeling on the large cushions, Delores and Savannah sat opposite, holding hands their bracelets started to glow, a vortex of extreme blue and white bright light started to engulf all four females, around and around the vortex travelled, pushing the high energy to the extremes, the vortex that engulfed the four women, travelling at an hypersonic speed, with flecks of rhythmic silver light flowing faster and faster, with fractured bolts of lightning forcing their way up through the vortex until there was an explosion, a massive bolt of energy and light blinding the four females.

Clearing their eyes all four women found themselves back in the combat training gym, gaining their senses, retrieving what resembles a Japanese Naginata, a long infantry weapon of the Samurai era, an ideal weapon for women, long handle with a curved blade on the end with immense cutting power, Sandra said "We will start with the wooden version before using a live blade", squaring off against Delores both women bowed to show respect to each other, Sandra and Delores took it in turns to attack and defend, with blow after blow, strike after strike, the training was intense, sometimes making contact with their bodies causing severe pain, gritting their teeth and sucking up the pain and carrying on like true warriors, It was the turn of Shireen and Savannah to face combat, with the basics already implanted in their brain it was polishing of their techniques, the same scenario, the same pain and gain was inflicted on each of the girls, strike after strike, contact after contact with each of the girls young bodies, both girls enduring the pain that they inflicted on each other was immense and severe, Delores clapped her hands and said with authority in her voice "ENOUGH", Shireen and Savannah looked extremely exhausted, Delores with a bemused look on her face said "Did you enjoy that ladies?", unknown to the girls Sandra had picked two crossbows, "Right ladies ,each of you take a crossbow", said Sandra, taking a crossbow each Shireen and Savannah looked bewildered as there was no string on the crossbow, Delores could see the bewilderment on Shireen and Savannah's faces, then said", Hold your bows like me", Delores struck a pose and the girls followed suit, each of the girls bracelets made contact with a brass terminals on the crossbow, making a full circuit brought they're bracelets to life, an extreme glow emanated from they're bracelets, a blinding sky blue and white light dazzled the entire room, in turn a same colour bow string appeared across the bow then an arrow straight afterwards in the same glowing colours, firing her crossbow at a target at the far end of the room, the unusual arrow from the crossbow obliterated the target, Sandra then said "It's time to have ago", both Shireen and Savannah fumbled on the first couple of shots then it became a second nature for both girls, while Sandra ordered Shireen and Savannah to put the their crossbows away, Delores barked the order to bring in the prisoners, Delores explained that before them stood spies from The Realm of the Dark Nexus, ordering the girls to pick-up a live blade Naginata each, then made their way to the spies at the far end of the room, then Delores then made the order to engage the spies, Shireen looked Savannah, Savannah looked at Shireen looked at Savannah in unison,charging at the spies from one end of the room to the other, as they arrived within 6 feet of the spies Shireen and Savannah raised their Naginata for the final thrust, so they thought, a large ball of electricity formulated at the edge of the Naginata, then there was a massive surge of energy and an enormous bolt of lightning discharged it's self from the Naginata, the massive ball of energy entrapped the spies and they disappeared into what could only be described as a black hole, the bolt of truth and justice disappeared into infinity, turning to Delores and Sandra Savannah "What happened there?", looking at each other Delores said "Well come to the bolt of truth and justice",

Shireen then asked, "What happens to them?", Sandra said" It's where they answer for their crimes

and re-education is inducted into they're DNA and brain", with a follow on question looking totally bewildered Shireen asked "How long do they spend being re-educated?", Delores replied "That my dear is depending on what has been decided by the bolt of truth and justice, how severe the crimes, decides they're penance and re-education by the bolt of truth and justice", from out of nowhere came "Bravo, Bravo", all four females turned their attention to this voice, Delores with a smile said" Ah, Master Jerome, a great surprise and pleasure", returning the compliment Jerome replied "The pleasure is all mine ladies, all of you are an elixir for sore eyes", Sandra replied "Smooth talker", then gave a flirtatious smile and giggle.

Shireen looking concerned said to Jerome "My uncle, where has he gone?", Jerome put his arm around Shireen and said "Your uncle is safe, he has had to go and deal with a few matters of state, he will be back very soon", smiling at Shireen said "No more worrying, your training must take precedence right now", nodding in agreeance Shireen understood that there was a lot more knowledge to acquire, wondering what else was about vex and surprise her very soul and mind, Shireen felt that trying to contemplate any future revelations right now, would only tax her mind and distract her from very purpose of her presence, in this realm of shrouded secrecy Shireen did not want hinder herself acquiring the skills and knowledge to become a Protector.

Jerome watched the ongoing attack after attack, defence after defence, watching from all angles, with the three instructors pushing the girls to they're limits, correcting their every move to perfection, the three instructors needed, wanted, demanded total obedience to their instruction, with relieve Jerome called out "Enough, time to replenish your young bodies", pointing towards a table behind them, walking across to the table sat five plates on the table, on the plate was a small meal, a slice of thick bread, fruit, meat and a drink of refreshing whatever it was, totally different taste that the girls had ever encountered, giving their taste buds a whole new experience, Shireen asked "What meat is this?", the three instructors looked at each other, Savannah looked inquisitively at the three instructors requiring her curiosity to be answered, Sandra then replied "It's meat but not a meat", Shireen thought here comes riddle time, Sandra went onto say "There are several vegetables that taste like different meats at the same nutritional value as meat", Sandra went onto explain how the vegetables were cooked reshaped as we knew the meat and re-cooked, Shireen asked "What do these vegetables what do they look like?,

Anticipating Shireen's question Jerome peeled back a cover to reveal several odd looking vegetables, the girls gazed at these vegetables, Jerome then said "you have done well, I will attend your last day of training", a further two days of intense arduous training took place, pushing Shireen and Savannah to the very core of their limits, their instructors Delores and Sandra, finding masses of encouragement and persuasion and enticement to exceed, on the last day of training, as promised Jerome turned up for the last day of training, watching enthusiastically, Jerome gazed with contentment that the instruction was to the highest level that could be expected, Shireen looked at light switch on the wall asked, "You have electricity?", Delores then said playing with the light switch "Your power comes by kind contribution of graginite and naganite, infused together gives light and portable heat, even weaponry, infusing different grades of graginite and naganite gives us different outcomes", Jerome finished his meal and drank the last of his fluids, looking at the four females said "You have made all made a tremendous effort in your training today, especially you two young ladies, Delores and Sandra, always a 100% from you two ladies in your instruction, I suggest that you bath and rest, tomorrow is your day of testing, you have had five moons of training, tomorrow is your day of reckoning, goodbye and good luck", Jerome walked with an awe of distinction to the other side of the gym, then disappearing altogether from view.

Holding hands and arms in what has become a regular occurrence of excitement and exhilaration, with all of their bracelets glowing intensely with the a shimmering bright sky blue and white light, the vortex encircled the women with the speed intensifying from one extreme to another, with the vortex totally engulfing the four women, travelling at hypersonic speeds, the colours of the vortex transcending from their bracelets, swirled around and around, flecks flowing like a swarm of silver coloured bees,

Bolts of thundering lightning shot from the bottom to the top at speeds that made hypersonic speed redundant.

Flash, bang and wallop the vortex disappeared, re-appearing in the quarters of Shireen and Sandra, the vortex gradually dissipated leaving all four women blinded momentarily, regaining their eyesight found themselves in familiar surroundings, found and liquid refreshments had already been to they're quarters, taking turns to bathe, finally sat down to have their meal, feeling completely refreshed and refuelled, re-energized, relaxed, nursed their aches and pains, Delores said "Before your final tests tomorrow you will learn to ride a Hossagon", Shireen and Savannah looked at each other with total shock and bewilderment, Shireen then said with a hint of hesitation in her voice and a she looked perturbed on her " What is a Hossagon ?", Sandra spoke before anyone else could say anything" Ladies the surprise is for tomorrow", smirking as she passed these words from her lips, a sudden movement from Delores raised herself up from the seated position from where she had made herself comfortable, then these words escaped her mouth, "Ladies, it's going to be a long day tomorrow, I suggest an early night", everyone nodded in agreeance, as Shireen and Savannah entered their bedroom, Sandra and Delores checked outside the door to their room, then outside the windows, making sure that the extra Palace guards were in place, fearing another kidnap attempt on Shireen, Delores and Sandra nodded at each other with satisfaction that all precautions were in place, the final comforting factor the noise of the wolf hounds and their handlers passing the windows.

As the night progressed, Delores and Sandra took turns on watch, alerting each other to the slightest rustle of the trees, noise of every animal, the changing of the guard, the sun finally started to rise to the delight of Delores and Sandra, turfing the girls out of bed, sitting down to their morning meal that had been delivered earlier, there was a knock on the door, opening the door the captain of the guard informed Sandra that all had been prepared for later, thanking the captain of the guard, Sandra closed the door, turning around to everyone in the room, then looked at Shireen and Savannah and said "Right ladies, a treat awaits the both of you", Then gave Delores a wink of her eye and smiled at each other, both girls looked at each other with scared but yet intrigued look of excitement.

What has become part of normality for the two young females and their instructors, was about to take place again, sitting in their usual formation, arms linked, their bracelets ignited with an intense glow of blue and white shimmer, static electricity filled the room, the vortex that they have come to know started to take form, the vortex intensified and intensified in speed, the height of the vortex increased rapidly followed in quick succession by the static electricity, speed, the effulgent of the vortex intensified in blazing brightness, the flecks of silver in the vortex pulsated around in the vortex in succession, as if it was visual binary code being typed by a super A.I. entity,

As the vortex engulfed the four females, the intensity of all aspects of the vortex reached a critical level, the progression of the vortex had reached the level that caused the four females to be blinded, a final enormous explosion of brightness like an afterglow of a nuclear explosion took place, after regaining their vision, found themselves in a field, Delores said to Shireen and Savannah "You have learned to use the power of the bracelets, to transport yourself away from harm, remember, this will use a lot of power in your bracelets", Sandra then said "Ladies use the power in your bracelets wisely, out there in the unknown, your bracelets could mean the difference between life and death, in the field stood two large white mares already saddled, the two mares trotted, that developed into a canter, reaching the four females, they demanded petting from the four females, by burying their heads into the four females armour clad bodies.

Sandra and Delores took the bridle of each horse, the bracelets on the two women started to glow, copper elements on the two horses bridle glowed, in unison with the bracelets of the two women and the copper elements of the horses glowed brightly, as if they had become one entity , transformations started to appear on the two horses, it was as if somebody had waved a magic wand, first the tails on the horses became longer developing scales, the hoofs transformed into claws, like a swing wing aeroplane spreading it's wings, a pair of wings spread out and upwards on whatever these creatures are about to become, finally half way up the neck of these creatures a dragons head took shape, Shireen and Savannah could not comprehend the transformations that their eyes had just witnessed, totally shocked, flabbergasted, bewildered, stunned, shocked, no word could fit the description of the enormity of the relevance of the transformation that had graced their eyes, each of these creatures took curiosity to Shireen and Savannah, Sandra and Delores allowing the heads of these creatures to travel forward, stood petrified as these creatures ventured closer and closer, Shireen and Savannah stood frozen, each of the creatures concerned came nose to nose with Shireen and Savannah, noses touching, the eyes of the creatures penetrating through the girls eyes straight into their minds of Shireen and Savannah, staring intensely hypnotising both females, without warning the two creatures pulled away, then thrusting forward laying their heavy heads on each of the girls shoulders, Delores said in her delectable Alabama voice "Don't be shy ladies, pet them like you would your dog", looking at each other, stroked the heads of the creatures, the creatures gave a deep heavy sigh of approval, Delores looked at Sandra, Sandra looked at Shireen, each of the women smiled at each other, then Sandra said "Well ladies I think you have made some new friends", Delores then said " Right, ladies these superb creatures are called Hossagon's, one on the right goes by the name of Egor, the one on the left is called Nadia, as you have experienced they are very friendly", then Sandra interrupted and said "Don't be fooled ladies these can be very ferocious entities when the occasion calls for their transformation".

Pulling on the reins of the of both Hossagon's, instructing

them to kneel down, pulling themselves up on the Hossagon's, both Sandra and Delores beckoned Shireen and Savannah to join them, climbing up and onto the Hossagon, Shireen sat in front of Sandra, Savannah sat in front of Delores, pulling on the reins both Hossagon's stood up, they started to flap their wings, as the Hossagon's increased the speed of their flapping of their wings, the intense flapping caused a tremendous draft that was like a sharp breeze on a winters day, with a slight kick of their heels and a pull of the reins gave the Hossagon's the que to take flight, the Hossagon's intensified the flapping of their wings, with a gallop and immense stretching of their wings, the Hossagon's took flight with their passengers onboard, increasing their altitude the Hossagon's started to soar through the clouds, with the odd flap of their wings to capture the thermals underneath their bodies, Shireen and Savannah were ecstatic, over whelmed by an experience they never ever envisaged happening, soaring down low, then soaring up high on the thermals beneath them, Sandra looked at Delores, Delores looked at Sandra, both women nodded at each other, leaning over the shoulders of two girls the words "It's your turn", scared the hell out of the two girls, reluctantly they both took the reins of the Hossagon's, the initial couple of minutes of their first time at the reins in charge of this magnificent beast, seemed to last a life time.

In succession Delores and Sandra instructed both Shireen and Savannah to pull back gently on the reins of the Hossagon, both Shireen and Savannah did as they were instructed; both Hossagon's descended towards the ground, flapping their wings to slow their decent as they came into land, both beasts lowered their bodies, before Shireen or Savannah could make any sort of move of their bodies, Sandra and Delores dis-mounted, both beasts looked at their mistresses, turning their heads and resting their heads on the shoulders of both women, petting the heads of both beasts Sandra said "Right ladies, it's your turn", smiling and petting the head of her Hossagon Delores said "Enjoy ladies", Delores then said to her Hossagon glancing over occasionally at Sandra's Hossagon" You two be gentle!, do you both hear me", both Hossagon's snuggled on either side of Delores's shoulders stroking their heads, their way of indicating that they understood, Sandra then said "Right, off you go", both girls pulling on the reins, indicated to the Hossagon's that the girls were ready to go, with a little dig of their heels and the pulling of the reins, set everything into motion, the Hossagon's extended their wings in unison, the Hossagon's flapped their wings, increasing the flapping of their wings steadily, then a little canter and both girls found themselves airborne, flying up and into the clouds, sunbeams cutting through the clouds, the wind rushing through both Shireen's and Savannah's hair, the constant rush of the harsh wind against the girls cheeks, made them glow a luscious pink on their young faces, zooming over hills and mountains, diving into deep ravines, both girls gripped onto the reins of the Hossagon with immense tightness, everything was stupendous, that was until Shireen's Hossagon felt danger in the air, Egor the Hossagon feeling all was not correct, Egor turned to Nadia, Nadia nodded to Egor, Delores and Sandra engaged in idle chit chat about anything and everything waiting for Shireen and Savannah, when both women descended into a trance with their bracelets glowing, the Hossagon through telepathy told Delores and Sandra of the imminent danger, Shireen and Savannah enjoying the most amazing time of their lives, seen their bracelets glow then the voice of Delores entered into their ears "It's Delores girls, rap the reins tight around your wrists, twist your feet in the stirrups and hold on as if your young lives depended on it", the voice of Sandra interrupted "We will get to you as soon as we can, let the Hossagon's do the flying", Both girls looked at each other, then did as instructed, turning to their right struck the fear of god at what they had witnessed, it was as if all the demons of hell was about to descend on the two girls and their Hossagon's, the two Hossagon's banked to their left and the true nature of their predicament unfolded, what looked like two flights of the most hideous creatures black hooded beings rode on their backs, these creatures, resembled a dragon, gleaming black scales from their noses to the very tip of their tails, the teeth they had could slice through any torso with easy of a knife slicing through soft butter, the sclera part of their eyes glistened like sparking diamonds, the iris of the eye was a deep blood red that pulsated, the pupil of eye was a dead black colour, after banking left the Hossagon's dived deep and low, Kris crossing each other with reek of death in hot pursuit, the Hossagon's flew deep and low on valley floors, pulling up and flying along the sides of the valley, these manoeuvres proved crucial in eliminating a couple of these creatures in pursuit, as they tried to intercept the two Hossagon's and passengers, not pulling up in time, sending their pursuers crashing and plummeting into the ground, slamming into the ground like a sledge hammer hitting a rock, the mixtures of lethal explosive gases and whatever substances laid within these creatures, exploded like a napalm bomb, sending an extreme heated fireball into the atmosphere, with a mixture of plumes of bellowing thick black smoke, with last of the red, orange flames entangled in the thick black smoke floated off into the sky, still in hot pursuit, the Hossagon's flew up and over the next mountain, descending at an extremely fast rate found themselves crossing a lake, using all the thermals they could muster, flew across the lake at a speed of a rocket, flying so low, the Hossagon's caused a large wake in the water, like a ship at full speed, the moist air caused a vapour trail coming from the tips of their wings, the pursuit was causing the Hossagon's to succumb to their tiredness, finally reaching the far end of the lake the Hossagon's landed in a clearing fully exhausted, Shireen and Savannah dis-mounted, drawing the swords from the scabbard's on their backs, their bracelets glowed an intense blinding blue, white light, it was their duty to protect Egor and Nadia, the two Hossagon's who had gone above and beyond the call of duty, trying to keep Shireen and Savanah from harm's way, on drawing of their swords, the swords took on the same bright glowing colour of their bracelets, the hoard that had been in close pursuit of Shireen and Savannah, landed, the riders and ferocious animals they rode descended within a hundred feet of the girls, dis-mounted, the hooded hoard fast marched towards Shireen and Savannah, stopping within fifteen feet of the girls, the leader of the hoard lifted his right hand, pointing his finger at Savanah and said in a deep dark voice "You are going to die, I'm going to enjoy watching you die", then this menacing demon turned in the direction of Shireen and said "You will come with me, you have been summoned by Queen Katarina, our mistress, the mighty one of the realm of the dark nexus", the girls looked at each other, turning to face each other, Shireen placed one sword against her thigh, the point of her sword pointing into the ground, placing her right hand on Savannah's cheek said "If we are going to die, we will die together", Savannah smiled with a tear in her eyes, then nodded with affection for Shireen's loyalty, picking her sword back-up, turned to face her fate, without warning, a jetted thrust of heated down draft passed over Shireen's and Savannah's head, followed by several bursts of intense prolific streams of fire, the streams of intense fire, burnt everything in its path, leaving the area in front of the girls, scorched, as the petrol smelling jets of fire hit the dragons, the dragons would explode like large thermobaric bomb making contact with their targets, the last of the sadistic looking savage beasts, had managed to evade the onslaught and barrage of a fiery death, pounded towards Shireen and Savannah, the beast lowered its head too tear the girls apart, the evil glistening eyes of the beast focused on the girls, Shireen and Savanah stood firm, within feet of the girls, there was blistering heated blast of a downward draft that flew all of the girls head, an almighty streak of fire raced across the sky, hitting the beast of a dragon square on the chest, the beast exploded into a million pieces, sending a massive fireball and shrapnel of the beasts scales flying in every direction, the blast projected Shireen and Savannah into the nearby undergrowth, the girls finally came too from the massive explosion a little while later, looking forward both girls could only see a blurred large scorched area, as Shireen and Savannah both steadied each other onto their knees, smouldering armour, cuts and bruises, still not able to focus properly, their Hossagon's just laid on the ground exhausted and shocked by the blast that they had endured, with their blurred eyes Shireen and Savannah saw two large creatures land with riders on their backs, Shireen turned to Savannah and said "Whatever happens, you will always be a dear friend to me", Savannah took Shireen's hand, then said "Dear friend", both girls smiled, closer and closer the two black clad beings drew closer, Shireen and Savannah gripped each other's hand, waiting to make the ultimate sacrifice, the two large figures finally stood towering of the girls, when a voice said "You're not going to learn much on your knees", breaking down into uncontrollable tears, Shireen recognised the voice of her uncle Marcus, grabbing hold of her uncle's leg, Shireen just sobbed, also present was Lord Chancellor Xander Blackstone helping Savannah to her feet, a few moments later the girls eyesight re-adjusted, seeing more clearly, heard an intense noise of flapping, Xander Blackstone turned to Marcus Greene and said "The cavalry has arrived ", turning back towards each other both men smiled and nodded, landing within feet of Shireen, Savannah, Marcus and Xander Blackstone, jumping of their Hossagon's and bolting towards them came Sandra and Delores, an entire squadron of Hossagon's flew overhead, surveying the aftermath that resembled an attack by a large destructive thermobaric bomb, everything in its path reduced to a cinder, charred debris everywhere, Sandra and Delores checking both girls over, coming to the conclusion, both girls battered and bruised bore no other combat wounds, all concerned went to check on the Hossagon's that bravely try to keep both Shireen and Savannah from the clutches of their foe, both Hossagon's gathered enough strength to stand up and started to walk around, Xander Blackstone gave instructions to one of the Army of Life officers, that both Hossagon's are to be walked for a while back to the Palace of Life, then flown the rest of the journey, the Hossagon's had changed fully back to their horse looking form, both girls were given instructions that they would travel back with Sandra and Delores, looking tearful, Delores looking at both Marcus Greene and Xander Blackstone said "I owe you everything I have for saving Savannah, that's wrong of me, for saving both of them", the tears streamed down the face of Delores like a torrent river, Sandra came a close second in the torrential tear contest, Delores hugged both men, wiping her tears off her face hugged Sandra, Sandra nodded and smiled at both Marcus and Xander Blackstone.

The clones received a message via the portal that brought them to the world of Marcus and Shireen Greene, the message said that they should prepare themselves to undertake any engagements, like the one family gathering looming, both clones then engaged in computing the information that flowed from the portal, the clone of Shireen stood up then entered the spare room where Shireen slept, going through Shireen's belongings gathering the DNA from Shireen's clothing, analysing the data from the DNA, the clone had a better understanding of Shireen's personality, the way she talked, the way Shireen walked, the way she thought, walking into the main room of the flat, the clone of Shireen met the clone of Marcus Greene, both clones had a better understanding of whom they represented.

Witnessing the total annihilation of some of her forces, through the eyes of her all spying blackbirds, Queen Katarina was far from amused, more so that the entity that was spread eagled in front of her in the air, bore the wrath of her anger, her nails extended to a needle point, then said "They think this is the end of my plans", then plunging her nails into her victim with tremendous vigour and hatred, her victim wretched in agonising pain, screaming that would send the shivers through the body of anybody or anything, then said "Then they are mistaken", lifting the chin of her latest bit of torture fun said "Me and you pretty are going to have a bit of fun, well for me it's going to be fun", then burst out into a blood curdling laughter as she inflicted more destructive bodily torture and agonising mental pain.

After climbing onto their Hossagon's, Shireen shared with Sandra, Savanah shared with her aunty Delores, the Hossagon's flapped and gave a little burst of a run then started to gain altitude, circling over the charred to a cindered area, both Shireen and Savannah felt a tear in the corner of her their eyes as they looked down, they felt that someone had definitely been looking out for them that day, that would be Master Marcus Greene and Lord Chancellor Xander Blackstone, flying over hilltops and mountains the flight of Hossagon's finally flew insight of the Palace of Life, descending to land by flapping their wings and extending their legs made contact with the ground, everyone dismounted from their Hossagon's and went about their duties, Shireen, Savannah, Delores, Sandra, Marcus and Xander Blackstone congregated outside of the main entrance of the Palace of Life, Shireen turned to Lord Chancellor Blackstone and said "I take it we have failed the training, I can only talk for myself, I would like you to reconsider if I have failed?", Savannah said "The same here Lord Chancellor", Xander Blackstone looked at Marcus Greene, Marcus Greene nodded in agreeance, turning back towards the girls Lord Chancellor Blackstone said "I am more than happy to accept you for inauguration tomorrow, the final acceptance will be made by the Beacon of Life, It's when your bracelets are infused by the beacon that has the final choice", Shireen and Savannah felt somewhat easier in the words of the Lord Chancellor, Delores said "Right, ladies bath and chow time", making their way to their accommodation, seeing the girls disappear into the Palace, Marcus Greene to Xander Blackstone and said "Tomorrow is going to be an interesting day", putting his hand on Marcus Greene's shoulder Xander Blackstone said "My friend, that is a sure thing".

CHAPTER SIX
TRUTH AND HONESTY

As the morning sun started rising, Marcus Greene took in the fresh morning air into his lungs, knowing that he owed his niece, Shireen, the honesty and truth she deserved about what he had learned at the White Witch Palace, most of all the importance she played in the plans of Queen Katarina, Marcus Greene thought to himself, before anything could be divulged the inauguration ceremony should take place, dressed in full Protectors uniform both Shireen and Savannah left their bedroom, looking both girls up and down, head to toe, Sandra and Savannah said" Perfect, absolutely perfect, right ladies show time, just listen to your instructions", making their way outside under Palace guard, marching across the lawn of the Palace, the drums of the Palace guard gave a beat that added to the excitement to the proceedings, making the entourage come to a complete halt stood Marcus Greene and Xander Blackstone, looking over both girls both Marcus Greene and Xander Blackstone gave their seal of approval, standing in front of Shireen, Marcus Greene placed his hands on Shireen's shoulders and said "I'm so proud of you", looking at Savannah Marcus Greene said "We are proud of both you", Xander Blackstone nodded at the captain of the palace guard, he then gave the order as both Shireen and Savannah found their place around the Beacon of Life, "Neophytes, present yourself", reaching palms outwards, one by one the successful Neophytes bracelets started to glow, being last to join the circle of life, the girls waited in anticipation, seeing a couple of the Neophytes not being accepted made the girls scared of being rejected, it came to Savannah's turn, with relieve her bracelets glowed intensely, last in the circle Shireen looked at her bracelets, there were a few moments of pausing, then out of nowhere Shireen's bracelets pulsated and shone brightly, all Neophytes placed their hands against the beacon, the sphere started rotate, the beacon started to pulsate a bright glowing white and blue light, the beacon looked as if it was melting then entwining around the limbs of the Neophytes, the sphere that hovered above the beacon rotated faster and faster, throbbing with an intense glow, the glow from the beacon reflected off the fast rotating sphere, like a large disco ball the flecks of light shot off in every direction, the static electric white and blue light melted through the Beacon, the Beacon then extended its self outwards like liquid jelly arms that entwined the Neophytes, the static electric white and blue light flowed through their bodies then escaped through Shireen's mouth, eyes, even escaping from Shireen's ears, Marcus Greene looked on proudly, Delores felt the same way, Delores took Sandra's hand and said "This would not have been possible without your help, thank you", Sandra smiled and said" It was a concerted effort", once the inauguration started to come to a close, the sphere's rotation slowed, the brightness of the beacon subdued, eventually the sphere came to a complete halt and the glow of the beacon faded, gaining their senses Shireen and Savannah hugged each other, they then noticed that their bracelets remained glowing, which made both girls so happy realising that they had really had been excepted by the Beacon, all the new Protectors made their way to their proposers, Shireen and Savannah were no exception to the rule, Xander Blackstone looked at Marcus Greene and said "You know what must be done", Marcus Greene looked at Xander Blackstone with some contempt, replying to Xander Blackstone "I'm well aware of what must be done", Xander Blackstone parted with the words before retiring to his quarters "Extend my congratulations to Shireen, and of course Savannah", turning around with the swirling of his Lord Chancellor robes, Xander Blackstone strolled into the palace, Marcus Greene kissed Shireen on the cheek and said "Well done, I'm very proud of you Shireen", turning to

Savannah, Marcus Greene congratulated Savannah, turning around sharply said to Shireen "We must talk later, enjoy the celebrations", taking Sandra and Delores too one side, all three entered into deep conversation, Shireen and Savannah hugged each other, taking an interest from a distance of the proceedings was Queen Katarina's blackbird spy, Queen Katarina had also viewed the proceedings through the blackbirds eyes, all of a sudden everything went blank, Jerome watching the proceedings from a distance, felt an uneasy feeling of being watched, his bracelets started to glow, saying to himself "I thought so", Jerome picked up his crossbow, the string on his crossbow glowed then a glowing arrow appeared, firing his crossbow he stunned the blackbird and the blackbird fell out of the tree, Jerome mounted his Hossagon to retrieve the blackbird, after a short ride Jerome reached the tree, jumping of his Hossagon Jerome picked up the stunned blackbird he had just shot with his crossbow, said to himself "So Katarina is at it again", Jerome rode back to the Palace of Life on his Hossagon at full speed, arriving back at the Palace of Life saw Marcus Greene talking to Delores and Sandra, with the wrapped up blackbird approached Marcus Greene and said "Excuse me ladies, I need the attention of Marcus", as both men walked away Jerome said to Marcus "We need to see Blackstone, something has turned up on our doorstep", opening up the cover Marcus Greene saw the blackbird had evil red eyes, Jerome said to Marcus "Where's Blackstone ?, In his study I presume", Marcus Greene replied, Entering the Palace marched towards Xander Blackstone's Study, turning the hallway Marcus Greene stopped Jerome and said "Myself and Blackstone intended to talk to you after the ceremony, things have now turned out differently", Jerome said to Marcus "How far am I in the loop things", Marcus Greene facing Jerome eye to eye said "You are the third person, I couldn't say anything until now, what I know, when I know, you will know, you are one of the closest friends I have", Jerome looking at Marcus Greene intensely said to Marcus "Time for a chat with Blackstone",

Shireen sat on her own not knowing how to feel, what to feel, the recent events made her grow quicker than she thought she would, looking deeply into her soul, realising that life would never, ever be the same again, Shireen looking down at her body armour, switching her eyesight from her uniform to her bracelets, felt immensely proud of herself, the only thing that Shireen knew she would have to do is keep her new life from everyone back in her realm.

Approaching Xander Blackstone's study both Marcus and Jerome found his door already open as if he was expecting the two men, entering his room they made straight for Xander Blackstone's desk.

Sitting down in front of Xander Blackstone, Marcus Greene to the left of him, Jerome then said "Right, who's going to enlighten me", then gave a cheesy smile, the big oak door slowly closed as the men went into conversation.

Finally deciding to much thought was not in her best interest, Shireen decided to make her way back to her room, from the corner of her eye Shireen noticed a female, she recognised the female dressed in a similar uniform yet it was a burgundy colour, not wanting to draw to much attention, Shireen kept on walking to her accommodation, as Shireen neared the entrance Shireen saw Egor and Nadia with Delores, looking over the Hossagon's Delores decided both animals looked to be in acceptable condition, smoothing the two Hossagon's thinking to herself, Delores said "Yes", Shireen bemused turned to Delores, smiling Delores said "Yes, you can take one for a flight, that's what you want", Delores then said "Stay around the area of the Palace, in fact I will come with you", taking the reins of Nadia Shireen's bracelets started to glow a white and blue colour, the copper plates on the bridle pulsated with the same glowing bright white blue light, the transformation of the Hossagon's began with the tail extending ridged, hoofs turning into a clawed paw, wings that protruded from the side of the Hossagon, the evolution of the head was the final part of the transformation of this magnificent creature, Shireen made the telepathic connection with Nadia, looking into each other's eyes, they both smiled at each other like old friends would, Nadia said "Let's have some fun", lowering herself down, Nadia lowered herself just a little more, enough that Shireen could climb into her saddle, turning that she could see Shireen out of one eye said "Where to?", Shireen replied "Nowhere far, just far enough", like a radio message being transmitted to both Shireen and Nadia Delores said "Remember what I said", both Shireen and Nadia looked at Delores and nodded, there was a little tug on the reins and Nadia knew it was time to fly, with the flapping of her wings intensifying and a skip and a little run, Nadia pulling her legs underneath her body, Shireen found herself airborne, Nadia said "Hold tight", wrapping her feet tightly in the stirrups, the reins tightly in her hands, Shireen gasped at the height they had achieved in such a short period of time, rising through the misty clouds, the wet mist on Shireen's face, bursting through the clouds into never-ending sunshine, soaring like a pair of eagles, Delores felt exhilarated just as much as Shireen, Kris crossing the skies, Kris crossing each other, then Nadia took a steep bank right and went into a deep dive with Delores and Egor in close pursuit, the pleasure and excitement that Shireen felt could not be explained into mere words, if words had to be used, fantastic, marvellous, stupendous, brilliant, these words could only become a mere fraction of the way Shireen was feeling, the wind blew Shireen's long blonde hair directly backwards, like a streak of blonde flames, finally levelling out flying over the tree tops low level, turning with the contours of mountains, flying as low as they could creating a vacuum underneath them making dust and debris fly in all directions, with massive intense flaps of her wings, Nadia's altitude increased rapidly thrusting both of them at great speed through the clouds, Delores keeping in close proximity of Shireen and Nadia, she then said to Egor "They think they can lose us", Egor just shook his head and gave what you would call a little chuckle, Soaring like the Queen of the clouds, Shireen didn't want this flight of exhilaration to end, Kris crossing over the clouds of what looked like cotton wool, riding just above the top of the clouds, then soaring up higher into the vast blueness of the sky, the inevitable order came from Delores to make their way back to the Palace, soaring at a gentle angle of decent through the clouds, like all good things come to an end so was this flight of fun about to do so, with the Palace grounds rapidly approaching, the Hossagon's gave a little flap of their wings to slow themselves down, with their legs fully extended they finally landed, lowering themselves down so their riders could dis-mount,this amazing the beast started its transformation back to resembling a horse, first the head, then wings, the feet and finally the tail changed in appearance, after the their conversation, the doors of Lord Chancellors study, with the final words coming from Xander Blackstone, everyone affected by this news, needs to be aware of the imminent danger they could be facing, both Marcus Greene and Jerome nodded towards Xander Blackstone, with the heavy oak doors closing, both Marcus and Jerome started to walk down the hallway, Jerome putting his right hand on Marcus Greene's shoulder said "that must of been one hell of a shock to the system", in a serious voice Marcus Greene said "It was, believe me it was, now to find Shireen", Jerome said "Yes, she is smack bang in the middle of it", Finally reaching the main doors of the Palace, the Palace guards opened the doors for Marcus and Jerome, turning to Jerome he said "Wish me luck", Jerome said "You don't need luck my friend, you have done nothing wrong, just tell it how it is, nothing more, nothing less, Shireen will understand", giving Jerome a muted smile headed for Shireen and Delores, reaching the two women enquired if they enjoyed their flight, both Delores and Shireen gave a big "YES", Marcus Greene turned to Delores and said "I need to have a chat with Shireen", taking the hint Delores said "See you both in a bit", Taking Shireen in a direction of a pagoda, Shireen asked her uncle "Is there anything wrong?", Marcus Greene stroking Shireen's back said "You have done nothing wrong, let's be clear about that, you may have become part of circumstances that you have no control over", sitting Shireen down on cushions in the pagoda Marcus Greene said "Take my arms into yours, I will show you rather than trying to explain to you", Shireen feeling apprehensive and somewhat scared, did as she was requested, taking hold of her uncle's arms, Marcus Greene taking hold of Shireen's arms both their bracelets making contact, the bracelets making contact, the blue and white glowing light intensified, a vortex started from the bottom of their bodies, rising around their bodies, getting faster and faster, with the speed and the brightness of vortex intensifying, the vortex finally engulfing both Shireen and Marcus Greene, the vortex found its self at the stage where the bright pulsating blue and white light became a blur, inside the vortex the bodies of Shireen and Marcus Greene became blurs to each other, a final blinding flash of light blinding both Marcus and Shireen, finding herself like an owl perched on someone's shoulder, looking to her left saw the face of her uncle, looking forward she could see Lord Chancellor Blackstone, it was as if she was watching a 3D TV, there was no sound, as if the mute button had been applied to the sound, both her uncle and Xander Blackstone are walking down a hallway, then seeing the Palace Guard coming to attention, doors being opened, in front ready to go there were two Hossagon's, both men climbed onto a Hossagon, Shireen could see both men look at each other, they nodded at each other than a pull of the reins and both Hossagon's took to the skies, flying high into the sky, flying over familiar territory, then a swirling massive looming worm hole drew closer and closer, reaching the edge of this what seemed to be a worm hole especially created for travel, entering the worm hole everything became an enormous kaleidoscope with bright white light patterns, with colours changing, shades of colours changing, patterns rebounding off each other, Shireen couldn't believe her eyes, witnessing such beautiful patterns and colours, they seemed to be in timeless motion, finally a bright light up ahead made it clear that their journey of bright lights and fantastic patterns are about to come to an end, reaching the end of the worm hole, both men had entered another realm, a bright white sun with the lightest of purple coloured skies, in the distance growing closer a tremendous throbbing , glowing white Palace, flying around the Palace, the Hossagon's started to flap their wings slowly, extending their legs, making a final approach, then landing in a court yard, Marcus Greene and Xander Blackstone dismounted, the Hossagon's reverted back to their horse like shape, the head, then the hoofs, the wings, finally the tail, there to meet them was an entourage of all white hooded beings, Marcus Greene and Xander Blackstone walked towards the waiting entourage, with Shireen's eyes taking every ounce of the picture unfolding in front of her, an aide formally introducing Queen Nadine of the White Witch Kingdom, pulling back her hood, revealed an auburn haired woman, green eyes like emeralds, ears with a slight point on top of the ears, the same height as Marcus Greene, moving as close as she could to Marcus Greene, clutching his hands said "My dear Marcus, it's been such a long time, Marcus Greene replied "Yes, it has been a very long time", still gazing into each other's eyes, as if they had lost each other in their very souls, Queen Nadine shook from the gaze of Marcus Greene's eyes and said "Let us go inside as we have matters of state to discuss, with burgundy uniforms stood the Palace guard coming to attention as the Queen entered the Palace, walking down a large hallway with portraits of previous queens, everything was a glistening bright white in the Palace, giving a feeling of warm, comfort and harmony, finally reaching a pair of large glittering white doors, the queens guard opened the doors, a room for entertaining heads of state, everything bright white, when the sun made contact with this room, the room would illuminate giving a warm vibrant feeling, Queen Nadine ordered everyone to leave except Marcus Greene and Xander Blackstone, as one set of doors closed another set opened, all eyes looked at the person who entered room, a young girl entered the room long dark hair, hazel eyes, roughly eighteen years old, dressed in a white glistening robe, Queen Nadine offered both men to sit down, Queen Nadine then said" This is Princess Joelle, my daughter, your daughter Marcus", Marcus Greene stood up so quickly it was like a taught spring had been unleashed from captivity , not sure what his next action should be, that was soon decided when his new found daughter walked towards her father and kissed his cheek, Marcus Greene kissed his new found daughter on the forehead, and said with tears of joy in his eyes "I had no idea", turning to Queen Nadine Marcus Greene said "Why didn't you tell me I had a daughter?", Queen Nadine told Marcus Greene that it was for the best for all concerned at the time, Shireen felt so happy for her uncle, he now had a child he thought he would never have, with tears of joy wondered how the rest of the family would react, would it remain a secret, sitting back down with his new found daughter sat at his side, looked at Xander Blackstone, looking into Marcus Greene's eyes Xander Blackstone then said "This is why I could not say anything to you my dear friend", Queen Nadine told Marcus Greene and Xander Blackstone of the story of how her sister Queen Katarina of The Realm Dark of Nexus, once an envoy became smitten with a young gorgeous prince of the dark arts, her sister had fallen for the dark side of witchcraft, finally the dark side took her soul over completely, first she tortured her love then killed him, taking over his kingdom, wanting more and more power, managing to give birth to three children, two boys, one girl, Astaroth, Lamia, Balor, aged roughly 21, 19 & 17, all the children had watched their mother use and abuse both men and women for her own sick perverse pleasure, casual sick perverse sex and torture reeked throughout the castle, making her victims in pain wished that someone would end their lives, instead a lingering death was all that awaited the poor souls, my sisters children are exactly the same, given their own enclaves they practice their own acts of perverse torture.

Queen Nadine said "One of the main reasons I called this meeting, is the lives of Joelle and Shireen are in immediate danger, when the three moons of Zerkon are about to align, with the right incantation and sacrifices, it will unleash demons and enhanced powers, that no thing or no one will be able to stop, Katarina has a new born child that one of her offspring has reproduced and being of White witch blood, Joelle has mixed blood from this realm and from your world Marcus that can draw in extra influencing powers, being the catalyst between two worlds, Shireen innocent like all involved will be the final link in the blood line, being of pure human blood is the final link, all three would be used as a blood sacrifice, they are connected by blood, as I see it, I think both girls should be kept together, that way they can be guarded, rather than stretching resources.

Queen Nadine said with a heavy heart "If all should fail then both girls must be executed, rather than fall into my sisters arms, that's how serious this matter has become".

 looking at each other Marcus Greene and Xander Blackstone agreed with Queen Nadine, Joelle said "Where am I to go?", Queen Nadine said "My dear daughter you will go with your father", turning fully said "I feel the defences at the realm of life can protect you better, as my sister may find a way back into our realm, as she once belonged to this realm of peace and tranquillity of the white witches ", with full agreeance of everyone, Queen Nadine said "You must be hungry and thirsty after your trip, please join us for evening meal, you can fly back first thing in the morning", Marcus Greene looked at Xander Blackstone, Xander Blackstone shrugged his shoulders and replied "Why not, a nice change of scenery", Queen Nadine then said "Joelle will show you to the guest rooms, I will make sure there will be guards on both rooms", Joelle said "Please come with me", both Marcus Greene and Xander Blackstone followed Joelle with an armed escort following close behind, walking down a vast corridor finally came to their rooms, Joelle said "Lord Chancellor this is your room", turning to Marcus Greene, smiled, then holding onto Marcus Greene's hands said "Father, this is your room, I will be back soon to collect you for your evening meal", Xander Blackstone said to Marcus Greene "A moment in private if you don't mind", Marcus Greene replied "Yes, of course", entering a room more like an apartment sat opposite each other, Xander Blackstone looking Marcus Greene straight in the eyes said "Can you now understand why I couldn't say anything to you, the up most secrecy had to be maintained", Marcus Greene said "So what now, are we to invade The Realm of The Dark Nexus, do we wait until they invade The Realm of Life?",

Xander Blackstone replied "It is up to the upper chamber to decide our fate, then the final decision will be made by the Beacon of Life, my own personal view, a full invasion would only antagonise other evil axis realms, creating a never-ending war", Xander Blackstone got up from his chair, place two goblets in front of him, poured two drinks, placing one in front of Marcus Greene then went onto say "Whether we like it or not we can only address the problems as they arise, Marcus Greene replied by saying "Fight them when they turn up", Zander Blackstone said "Very much so", Xander Blackstone said "One battle at the time", Marcus Greene agreed, finishing his drink, Marcus Greene said "Time to freshen up".

Queen Katarina gazed out of her Palace window, looking down into the courtyard. Marching out into the courtyard, twelve or so Turgan mercenaries, Turgan's, a form of large gruesome looking elves, they thought they had seen an opportunity to sneak into the Palace, kill Queen Katarina and her offspring and take control of her realm.

Little did they know, one of their so-called band of mercenaries sold them out for a large reward, a trap was set and all participants were captured, the noise of large doors being opened underneath the Palace echoed around the courtyard, as the Turgan's looked into the dark lair, all they could see was sparking diamond sclera's, pulsating blood red irises, these intense menacing eyes drew closer and closer, faster and faster, until the Zorgar dragons finally escaped their lair, hysterical cries rung out, clutching onto a scarlet coloured curtain, Queen Katarina trembled and shaked violently with excitement and anticipation, as she watched the chaotic frenzy of the Turgan's take place, everyone for themselves, listening to the screams was like listening to a favourite piece of music for Queen Katarina, pivoting and dancing to the screams of infliction swirling around and around, the strongest Turgan's threw their less capable comrades at the approaching dragons, the Zorgar's biting and gnawing of flesh and bone echoed around the enclosed courtyard, as the Turgan's offered up for sacrifice screamed in agonising pain and suffering, being mutilated and disfigured embraced their death as a release, the Turgan's that tried to run in some form of direction, met a second wave of Zorgar's.

These Zorgar's had a more acquired taste and flambeed their Turgan's, still alive, burning flames engulfing their bodies, wriggled in torturous, agonising pain, from their taught tight bodies, fat oozed from the splits in their skin, as if they were basting their own bodies, they suffered no more once they had their bodies torn and ripped apart and finally devoured, all that remained was a scorched, spattered blood stained courtyard, closing the balcony doors contemplating if her plan of total rule would succeed, turning waving her hands transforming herself from an evil looking witch into a lovable innocent looking female, dressed in a white flowing solstice dress, fair hair, looking at all of her off-spring Queen Katarina said "Is everything in place?" all three children replied "Yes mother".

Queen Katarina looking straight into Lamia's eyes, a sadistic soul just like her mother, Queen Katarina looked at her offspring as they sat on chairs fit for kings, Queen Katarina stared at the wall of hate, the wall of hate was a large crude oil black colour with a high definition sheen finish, every time Queen Katarina became enraged a voice would echo and repeat her very words, a shimmering head would also appear as Queen Katarina's anger intensified, the wall of hate hid Queen Katarina's deepest secrets, looking around the high ceiling quarters, at the many portraits that hung on the wall opposite the wall of hate, admiring the implements of torture, suffering and of excruciating pain, walking behind her offspring, dragging her exceptionally sharp and lethal nails along the back of the wooden chairs, that could shred the human body into a thousand pieces, causing fear amongst her children, changing back into her clothes of evil as she walked, her hair changing from innocents into black exceptional evil, the wall of hate echoed Queen Katarina's words of warning, the wall of hate sent a shimmering image that followed and echoed her words, "We have already had one failure, I don't expect another one",.

The shimmering image that followed Queen Katarina reiterated her very words, sending a frightening chill up the spine of her off-spring Lamia said "My dear mother, it was Astaroth's troops that failed".

Balor the Queen's youngest off-spring sniggered as his older siblings bore the wrath of their mother, turning and glaring into the eyes of Balor, Katarina then said to Balor, "My child you find it amusing how I scold your older siblings, remember this if there is any more failures, I will punish you all equally".

Balor sat in front of his mother all sullen after his scolding, Queen Katarina then turned her back on her offspring, then said "Leave me now, heed my warning, you know the consequences if you fail me", the shimmering image that escorted Queen Katarina disappeared back into the wall of hate, walking over to a table of torture, laid stretched out on a table was a young girl, a pixie looking girl chained to the torture table, dressed as a scantily clad serving girl, her bosom heaving up and down rapidly, the heaving of this young females bosom increased every time Queen Katarina ran her nails over her young body, the young girl could not even wriggle in pain if she wanted too, Katarina said to the young girl "Don't be scared my dear, the first bit will be pleasurable for the both of us, however the second part of our little get together, well, let's just say that's going to be my ultimate climax to the evening", as Katarina ran her sharp nails from tip to toe of the young girl body, catching her nails now and again in her clothing.

Prince Astaroth, he stood six feet tall, broad chest, jet black swept back hair, every young girl's fantasy lover, evil and sadistic just like his mother, they say that the poisonous apple does not fall far from the tree.

Princess Lamia, she stood just short of five feet eight tall, certainly a chip off the old block, her sexual preferences was just about anything, however she did have a little bit more of an interest in girls her around her own age.

Prince Balor, five foot ten, spitting image of his older brother, he just participated what everyone else was indulging in, a true family member.

There was a knock on Marcus Greene's door, then a knock on Xander Blackstone's door, both doors simultaneously, outside their doors stood Joelle, her adorable voice said "Please follow me gentlemen", leading Marcus Greene and Xander Blackstone into a banquet room, smiling at both Marcus Greene and Xander Blackstone, Queen Nadine then announced "This banquet is in honour of our special guests", there was applause from the guests that were in attendance, the evening went smoothly, Marcus Greene stood out on the balcony admiring the three sky blue moons, Joelle could see her new found father on his own, clasping her father's arm, Marcus Greene then put his arm around his daughter, Joelle said "We have a lot of catching up to do".

Marcus Greene replied "Yes, we certainly do", Joelle then asked could she stay with him in his human world, Marcus Greene then said "The big question is can I obtain permission, the two councils and the Beacon of Life, they might not grant permission for you to see my world, looking up at her father, Joelle said "I presume all has been decided, that's the impression the Lord Chancellor and my mother have negotiated", Marcus Greene just shook his head and laughed, watching Marcus Greene and Joelle together, he guessed that Joelle had just spilled the beans,.

Xander Blackstone decided to have a quiet word with Marcus Greene, feeling a presence behind him Marcus Greene turned around, so did Joelle, Marcus Greene then said "Did you forget to tell me something?", Xander Blackstone put his hands up and said "Guilty as charged, with everything going on, I did honestly forget "both men shook hands, Marcus Greene then said "Easily done my friend, please if there is anything else that comes to mind, inform me straight away", The night came to a close everyone made their way to the rooms allocated, Shireen watching the evenings events unfold before her could not believe what she was witnessing, the fact of the matter she had had to come to terms, she had a new cousin, was it a fact that this family member might have to stay in the wardrobe,.

Shireen still feeling she was an invisible owl, she felt there was more secrets and truths to be exposed, wait and watch was the only way to go forward, Shireen felt that her uncle had been more than honest the whole of her life, in fact her uncle had put his cards on the table, letting Shireen see Marcus Greene's thoughts was the ultimate trust that one person could show another person, drifting off again into Marcus Greene's thoughts, she could see her uncle and the Lord Chancellor in conversation, it was decided that both men would stay until a couple of moons had passed, treaties would be discussed and ratified, Marcus Greene would spend time getting to know his new found daughter, Marcus Greene sat with his daughter, a warm breeze bustled around father and daughter as they discussed, their lives, their two very different worlds, Joelle then informed her father Marcus Greene, she had already visited his world, how Joelle sought him and Shireen out, Marcus Greene said "I know you had visited, I felt your presence, I didn't know, who, what or why, I just felt a close presence", Joelle then told Marcus Greene how Joelle and Shireen's paths had crossed in the martial arts shop.

Marcus Greene soon realised that so many boxes had been ticked, in such a short period of time, the jigsaw pieces were fitting, Shireen as she watched with intense vigour, realised that her video jigsaw was nearly complete, there only remained a few pieces to complete her jigsaw, as all good things do, it came to an end, it was time for Marcus Greene and Joelle to part company, all they knew that they would be reunited very soon, spending the morning together enjoying a stroll, before Marcus Greene departed back to the Realm of Life, Marcus Greene felt that time had robbed him of the joys and tribulations of being a father, the experience of witnessing Joelle's first of everything, achievements, disappointments, all Marcus Greene knew is that the past needed to stay in the past, looking forward, not to forward, just enough for something to look forward too, enjoying all that would present its self before the two of them, Marcus Greene thought to himself, if Joelle has been allowed by the two chambers and the Beacon of Life, to visit his world then maybe there is a possibility for Joelle to stay with himself, under the pretence of being a tenant, the possibility of this scenario was not as farfetched as Marcus Greene first thought, a final meeting was arranged before Xander Blackstone and Marcus Greene departed, the full white witch council would be attending, morning refreshments had just started to be served, fruit punch was offered to all that attended The Great Hall of Wisdom, Truth and Integrity, a high ceiling room, exquisite art on each of the four walls, marble floor slabs with grey flecks, graced from one end of the room, to the other side of the room, red oak oval table with the centre removed, matching red oak chairs in the centre of the Great Hall, above their heads, a painted ceiling of a giant white owl, preferred mode of transport as broomsticks can be a bit uncomfortable, the usher of the council called order, the captain of the guard gave the order for The Great Hall doors to be closed, the heavy wooden doors closed with a "clunk", taking their seats, Queen Nadine brought the council to order, then introduced her guests.

Lord Chancellor Blackstone and Marcus Greene, who sat on either side of Queen Nadine, in her speech Queen Nadine told the white witch council, that although the kingdom was predominantly witches and their families, the kingdom was proud to take in refugees from realms where persecution and torture reined.

All of these refugees had made the kingdom their permanent ome, adding to the prosperity and secu rity of the kingdom, Queen Nadine came around to thanking The Realm of Life, for their co-operation in security and trade, reminding the council members that everyone played a part for safety and security for each other, no one should be under the misconception that all is safe.

Queen Nadine then announced that further treaties in

trade and security had been signed, it was also announced that envoys would be sent to other realms, the purpose of the envoys was to encourage other realms to sign up to an alliance, an alliance that would protect all, some council members seemed sceptical in these alliances, for need of the alliances, Queen Nadine soon addressed their concerns by saying "Knowing that we have friends willing to help us in possible times of need, will only give us all added protection and security, be alone and we will perish, all of us act as one, then we have a future".

Queen Nadine invited Lord Chancellor Blackstone to say a few words, thanking Queen Nadine for her hospitality, Xander Blackstone went on to thank the council for their generosity, reminding the council that Queen Nadine was a woman of great perception and hindsight, he reminded the council that acting alone would only make the realm more vulnerable, acting as one consortium would vastly reduce acts aggression from outside sources, finishing his speech, Xander Blackstone once again thanked everyone for their generosity.

As the final goodbyes took place, Marcus Greene looked at his once beloved and said " Until the next time", Queen Nadine replied "Let the next time be soon".

Parting clasps of hands and kisses, the walking down the corridors of power came the inevitable goodbye was close, leading out onto the courtyard where they first arrived stood the Hossagon's fully transformed.

Xander Blackstone turned to face Queen Nadine, thanking her again for her hospitality, Queen Nadine said "Princess Joelle would arrive in a couple of days under escort", Xander Blackstone replied "I will look forward to the Princesses arrival, the necessary arrangements would be made".

Both Marcus Greene and Xander Blackstone bowed out of respect for the Queen, The two Hossagon's lowered themselves so that Marcus Greene and Xander Blackstone could take to their saddles, placing their feet in the stirrups and taking control of the reins, a final wave and goodbye, a slight nudge of their heels and the Hossagon's flapped their wings intensely and with a short run found themselves increasing altitude. Gaining height, circling the white witch palace then made directly for The Realm of Life,.

With their feet tucked beneath them and an odd flap of their wings, the Hossagon's soared at great speed, it was about the time that Marcus Greene and Xander Blackstone were about to fly over the Draggor mountains, they intercepted the distress telepathy message from Delores to Shireen and Savannah.

Both men looked down to their right, only to the hoard of Zorgar's and their riders in pursuit of Shireen and Savannah, pulling on the reins of the Hossagon's, they descended to engage the Zorgar's and their riders, The Hossagon's could see battle was about to commence, stoking up the bellows, the fiery cocktail smell of petrol and gases embraced the noses of both men, banking to the right then going into a steep dive both Marcus and Xander could see the fast approaching mass of black on foot reach the two girls, flying in low and fast, the first fiery bursts from both animals struck their foe, explosion after explosion erupted as they hit their targets, making a sharp left hand turn with the vapour trails coming the tips of their wings, the Hossagon's lined up for another attack, Marcus Greene and Xander Blackstone viewed the results of their attacks on their foes, could see that only one Zargor remained, they could see the Zargor lining up, then viewed the Zargor begin it's at charge at Shireen and Savannah, swooping in low and as fast as they could, both Hossagon's released a continued and intense burst of fiery death, the fiery blast engulfed the last Zargor, hitting the Zargor square on, the Zargor exploded into a fireball of a million pieces, plumes of smoke and fire escaped into the atmosphere, coming out of her so vivid dream Marcus Green said "Well, you know the rest of the story",

Queen Katarina looked up into the night sky, Queen Katarina could see the three moons of Zerkon, they had started aligning, swirling rainbow clouds started to form around all three moons, the anticipation of her desires of total supremacy, drifted around and around her ever scheming mind, if all was successful where would she strike first, who would be her first victim of torture and fun, changing her attire which looked like a leather clad pirate with thigh high boots, with a swipe of her hands, her attire slowly disappeared replaced by a long black soft lace dressing gown, Queen Katarina laid on a large leather sofa, snuggling into very large cushions, snapping her fingers a freshly laid log fire lit itself, then her body guards arrived in the form of two black panthers, laying down on a rug in front of the fire, Queen Katarina drifted off to sleep with a smile that extended from one ear to the other, whilst Queen Katarina slept in another part of her Palace, her offspring conspired well into the night, thrashing out plans and details, tiredness had beaten the evil conspiring siblings, making their way to their quarters, a final nod in agreeance then disappearing into their quarters.

CHAPTER SEVEN
TIME WILL TELL

Xander Blackstone sent for Marcus Greene and Jerome, after receiving their invites both men arrived simultaneously at Xander Blackstone's study, the doors of his study already open, sat at his large magnificent gleaming desk, Marcus Greene and Jerome felt an extra presence in the study, before Marcus Greene or Jerome could utter any words, Xander Blackstone said" Gentlemen we have a guest", Marcus Greene replied "We guessed there was an extra presence, White witch variety", a voice then sounded out from a chair facing a fire place "Father, lovely to hear your voice so soon", getting up from her chair Princess Joelle got up from her chair, dressed in a uniform much the same as the three men in the room, except it was a burgundy colour, walking towards her father, cwtching him, then kissing him on the cheek, looking at Jerome, Joelle said "Who is this fine man", Marcus Greene smirked and said "This my dear is Master Jerome", Cwtching Jerome, Jerome said "This lady must have your brains, she certainly doesn't have your looks, that would have been a curse on the poor girl", that comment even made Xander Blackstone lay back in his regal chair and laugh.

Marcus Greene then said to Joelle "You might as well meet your cousin, that's with the Lord Chancellor's permission", Xander Blackstone said "We have a meeting with the lower chamber, we can do the introductions along the way", Jerome led the way down the long wide corridor, finally reaching a door on the right, Jerome knocked the door, Delores called out "Who is it?", Jerome in one of his witty moods said "It's me honey, I'm home", opening the door

Delores said "My, my, so many visitors", entering Shireen's quarters Marcus Greene said "Well everyone this is Princess Joelle, please introduce yourselves", the introduction went around the room, then it came to Shireen, Joelle looked at Shireen, Shireen looked at Joelle, Shireen said "We have met before", Joelle in quick succession of answers with Shireen said "We certainly have, cousin", cwtching Shireen, both girls stood back admiring each other, interrupting Xander Blackstone said" While we are all together, a plan has been formulated", everyone listening intently, Xander Blackstone then informed everyone in that with Shireen's and Joelle's permission they would be used as bait, the three moons of Zerkon had nearly aligned, instead of waiting for an ambush they would seize the initiative and set their own ambush, this had been agreed by the lower and upper chamber's, the keeper of the beacon had relayed a message that the Beacon had approved the plan, Queen Nadine and the White witch council had approved the ambush, Xander Blackstone then said "Ladies it all rests on your decision", looking at each other both Shireen and Joelle said "Count us in".

Marcus Greene wasn't exactly happy about using his niece and new found daughter to flush out spies of the Queen Katarina, Marcus Greene realised that there was no easy way of evading this predicament that stood before everyone. Calling Xander Blackstone and Jerome to one side said "I need to see the both of you".

Feeling this could be a lengthy conversation Xander Blackstone said, "My study it is, gentlemen follow me", Xander Blackstone turning and looking at all five women said " Ladies if you would be so kind to excuse us, we shall return with a full plan and details of tomorrows fun packed day of enthralling entertainment".

All five women looked stunned at Xander Blackstone's attempt at jovial satire, closing the door behind them, all three men walked towards Xander Blackstone's study, stopping in the hallway Jerome said to Xander Blackstone "So how are we going to lure out this kidnap raiding party of Queen

Katarina?", Marcus Greene and Xander Blackstone had the same idea at the same time, a Deja vu moment between the two men, Blurting out at the same time," The blackbird", the blackbird that Jerome had stunned had been put in small Avery on its own, still connected to her mistress, the three men devised a plan of deception and capture, worst case scenario death would be the final option for the perpetrators of such an attempt.

Walking through an entrance at the rear of the palace, the palace guard came to attention, roughly thirty feet away in an Avery of its own was Queen Katarina's blackbird spy, stopping in front of the Avery, turning in the direction of Marcus Greene and Jerome, Xander Blackstone said to the two men, " That's decided, Shireen and Princess Joelle will patrol the market in the town tomorrow", Jerome then said "Are you sure it's safe for the two girls", Marcus Greene interrupts and says " I hope you know what you are doing?", Xander Blackstone replies in a stern and authoritarian voice, "We can't keep holding their hands, they have become Protectors of the Beacon of Life, then let them behave like one, walking away, around the side of the palace, Jerome said to Marcus Greene and Xander Blackstone, "That should do it", all three men laughed as they walked underneath an archway, looking through the window Shireen could see the three men, that is when Shireen had a flashback to an earlier vision she had experienced, quivering as she stood, Shireen could see her video jigsaw was finally falling into place, all that was required was the final pieces.

Queen Katarina came out of her trance, she had just witnessed the conversation and the scolding that Xander Blackstone had dished out to Marcus Greene, sat in a bath made for four, scented bath bubbles and candles surrounded Queen Katarina's body, closing her eyes and having the feeling of satisfaction that an opportunity had presented itself, laying back in her bath, dragging her nails along the side of the bath, she thought to herself YES, a feeling of desire of self-sexual gratification intensified and shrouded her body,

A war council had been arranged for all involved in the planned capture of enemies of the Beacon of Life, it was a risky plan to say the least, only high ranking of the Palace guard knew of the plan, everyone concerned from Shireen and company to Marcus Greene and Jerome were summoned to a ward room, Xander Blackstone called the war council to order, Taking to his feet Xander Blackstone said "Right, everyone knows their part in our plan, secrecy must be kept to the up most, don't forget you are the actors and the play you are performing must be faultless, it believable, one whiff of incompetence and all will be lost", looking around the room Xander Blackstone then said " I suggest everyone has an early night, tomorrow is going to be an exceptional day", everyone drifted out of the ward room, Xander Blackstone called Marcus Greene back into the room, he then said "I know you have a lot to lose with this plan, a niece, a daughter, It's better we control any type of kidnap attempt, rather than one we don't know about, when and where to expect such an attempt ", knowing that Xander Blackstone was right, a true friend, not always seeing eye to eye, Marcus Greene had every faith in Xander Blackstone's preparation for the military operation that was about to commence, Xander Blackstone said to Marcus Greene " Why don't you sit down, I will pour us a drink", pouring two large glasses of liqueur, Xander Blackstone placed a drink in front of Marcus Greene, then made a toast "Here's to you, here's to me, here's to Queen Katarina kissing my ass", both men burst out laughing, Shireen laid in her bed tossing and turning, thinking with some apprehension, getting out of bed gazing up at the moon, trying to perceive the outcome of forth coming events waiting to take place, finally getting back into her bed and drifting off to sleep.

Queen Katarina gave orders that all her offspring should attend her chambers first thing in the morning, laying in a large comfortable bed, dressed in a black satin dressing gown and little else, from no-where appeared her fearsome black panther body guards, they purred as they laid either side of her bed, Queen Katarina laid in her bed trying to devise a plan in her vile, evil, sadistic mind, finally drifting and scheming off to sleep, fantasizing of the ritual that is going bestow her to rightful position of Queen of anything and everything, Queen of all known worlds, realms and universes.

Shireen woke up to see Princess Joelle sat in a chair, resting as if she was in a trance, keeping a watchful presence over her new found cousin and Savannah, Savannah woke-up, looked around her and saw everyone in the room awake, laying her head on the soft pillows, Savannah rested with thoughts of contemplation on the nearing day's events that would take place, nobody could really sleep just resting their eyes, occasionally dropping off to sleep, as Shireen made her last toss and turn in her warm bed, there was a knock on the door, then the door opened up, Delores entered the bedroom and said, Right ladies, time to put down your teddy bears and whatever else you may be holding in your dreams, time to get up, it's a lovely day", smiled and left the room.

Dressed in a long flowing black silk dress, her crown that had many colourful fixations attached to it, perched on Queen Katarina's head, an array of different types of make-up had been applied to the Queen Katarina's face,

Queen Katarina sat on her chair of office, she sat on her throne of complete obedience and dominance , from everyone who had the miss-fortune to fall under her realm and enclaves of her rule, Queen Katarina's court doors opened up, it was all three of her off-spring, flanked by the Palace guard they walked towards Queen Katarina, bowing in homage to their mother, Queen Katarina then said "You may sit", informing her off-spring of the information she had received from her blackbird spy, the plan Queen Katarina devised was explained to her off-spring, also explaining that there was only one opportunity remained to succeed, the moons of Zerkon are about to align completely, Queen Katarina reminded her off-spring that they would not align for some time to come, if they missed this opportunity then life would be very uncomfortable for all of them, her off-spring reminded her that she asked them to devise a plan, Queen Katarina told her children that was no longer required after the last fiasco her plan was the one to be adhered too, she then ordered her off-spring to leave and carry out her instructions, Queen Katarina ordered her palace guard to close the doors to her court, that is when Queen Katarina rethought the full details of the capture of Shireen and Princess Joelle.

Leaving their quarters all five women walked down the corridor to the entrance of the Palace of Life, there was a unreal presence in the air, feeling self-righteous, a defined feeling of right against wrong, good against evil, Shireen was experiencing unknown parameters of a world of extreme differences, finally making it to the entrance of this massive palace, two Hossagon's awaited, the Hossagon's stretched forward so both Shireen and Joelle could climb into their saddles, there to greet them was Marcus Greene, Xander Blackstone and Jerome, all three men gave their last words of divine wisdom, Xander Blackstone assuring the young girls that there would be more than adequate protection around them, Jerome stepped forward and said "Did tight ass Blackstone give you any coinage ?," both girls laughed and said "No" Jerome looked at Xander Blackstone and shook his head, Xander Blackstone shrugged his shoulders and said "I can't think of everything" then smiled, Jerome then produced two pouches, giving both girls a pouch each containing coins.

Jerome's whit broke the girls and everyone's nervousness, Marcus Greene stepped forward separating the two large Hossagon's, clasping one hand each Shireen and Joelle, kissing the hand of his niece and his daughter then said "Just play your part, we will all be there to protect you", don't forget to call and see the keeper of the log, looking at the whole of these emotional proceedings stood, Delores, Sandra and Savannah, parting words from Delores came in the words of " Don't do what I wouldn't do", Jerome turned his head and said " That doesn't leave a lot", finally saying his last goodbye's the girls Hossagon's trotted away towards the entrance of the Palace of Life.

The guards opening up the great large fortified gates of the palace, before finally leaving the palace grounds out of sight.

Both girls looked back for one last time, giving a final farewell, then disappeared. both Shireen and Joelle looked at each other, Shireen then said " It's just me and you now girlie", Joelle replied " Don't worry I'm sure we are being watched and well protected as we speak", Princess Joelle was correct in her assumptions, overhead flew a black crow, what none of them knew is that Xander Blackstone had ordered the special guard of life, a highly trained company of guards, to shadow Shireen and Joelle's every move, hidden in the woods that lined the road to the town, the special guard made their way through the woods on armoured Hossagon's. Flying high in the sky out of view was an extremely large owl, the eyes of the owl relayed visions back to Queen Nadine, someone was watching something or someone, the only one who was unaware of what was happening was Queen Katarina, the closer the girls got towards town, the trap tightened on Queen Katarina's off-spring and spies, closer and closer, the town came into view, like warriors of the night the special guard of life watched from a distance.

The blackbird spy disappeared by the order of Queen Katarina, she did not want to draw any unnecessary attention, grasping at her heavily heaving bosom, her heart beating twice as fast, Queen Katarina could feel her desire of being Supreme Queen of all realms that could be travelled. Once the ceremony of the three moons of Zerkon had been completed, the ecstasy that gripped this demon in this females body was as if she had achieved multiple sexual orgasms all at once.

laying down on the large leather sofa with extra-large cushions, falling into hypnotic trance and afterglow, her black panther body guards took up their usual positions, stretching out on the large rugs they had be allocated, the black panther body guards slowly closed their eyes and went to sleep, their ears still listened out for any sudden noises or intruders, the company of the special guard of life took up positions around the outskirts of the town.

Entering the town on their Hossagon's Shireen and Joelle felt an uneasy presence, coming to a complete stop at the edge of the market, the two girls ordered their Hossagon's to lower themselves down, once the Hossagon's had lowered themselves the two girls got off their Hossagon's, they went straight to the keeper of the log's town's office.

The keeper of the log was an individual who kept a log of unusual occurrences that had happened in the town. Opening up the door to the keeper of the log's office, stood in front of them was a antrian, nearly seven feet tall, nearly as wide, human looking apart from a split in the centre of their bottom and top lips. An ex- Protector wearing the same style uniform in a dark sea green colour.

Feeling their presence the antrian looked around and said "Ah, protectors come to check the log", Shireen replied "Yes, we are", The antrian replied" Just fresh out of the training", Joelle then replied "Yes we are", the antrian replied again "My name is Atmos", the girls introduced themselves "My name is Shireen", "My name is Joelle", placing the log on the desk in front of Shireen and Joelle, Atmos said "There have been a few new faces in the town, opening up the log on the day's concerned, they played out like a 3D video, taking note mentally, Shireen said to Atmos" Do you know where these individuals are right now", Atmos replied " That's the strange thing, the log has lost contact with them, I have my suspicions they are from the Realm of the Dark Nexus, Joelle then said "Time for a little look around", Atmos said "Do be careful ladies" Shireen and Joelle said "Thank you", Atmos replied "Nice to see you, do call again", Shireen replied "Nice to meet you Atmos", Joelle just smiled and nodded, closing the door of the log keepers office Shireen and Joelle walked towards the market, Shireen said to Joelle "Time to contact my uncle", Joelle nodded in agreeance, placing her bracelets together, Shireen then called her uncle through telepathy, Shireen explained to Marcus Greene what they had discovered at the log keepers office, Marcus Greene advised both girls to keep a low profile, both girls knew that if anything was to occur that adequate protection would be nearby,.

What Shireen and Joelle didn't know how close that protection was, already in place and ready to spring into action, the special guard of life had just finished off surrounding the town, waiting in the woods ready to pounce on any perceived threats that may try and kidnap or harm Shireen and Joelle, sending her crow spy for a last sweep over the market area, Queen Katarina watched her off-spring place themselves in appropriate positions ready to acquire their prizes, Queen Katarina hoped that the day's military style operations would be executed fully, blinking her eyes twice Queen Katarina's blackbird spy found a perch on a roof top overlooking the market, the blackbird kept all-round vigilance of the immediate area, making sure there was not about to be any security breaches against the intending snatch squad.

Shireen and Joelle strolled around this extensive market, admiring various item's Shireen and Joelle had never set eyes upon until this very day, perusing stalls and shops of every culture, realm and race only known to those that visited this market of wonder, spiralling worm holes would appear of those arriving and those departing, from a variety of different foods to herbal medicines, soothing oils for aching bodies, Shireen and Joelle were being offered all sorts of phenomenal mouth-watering samples, Joelle then spotted a distinctive looking purple fruit, Joelle tugged at Shireen's arm and said "Look", as Joelle pointed at this amazing concept of stomach filling delight out to Shireen, as they grew closer and closer to the market stall, they could see this fruit which contained fruit, it could only be described as a very large purple strawberry with little purple strawberries growing on the outer skin, stopping at the stall admiring this piece of art, then a young voice from behind the two girls said "That looks exquisite, juicy, delightful, enough for three to enjoy".

Unknown to the girls they had now made contact with Princess Lamia, Princess Lamia was dressed in a deep emerald green, swirling dress with matching cloak and satin gloves. Shireen and Joelle looked at each other, they knew they were in trouble as cloaked individuals started to make a half circle around the two girls.

Princess Lamia had a ring on either hand with a needle dipped in a strong sedative drug, Princess Lamia walked towards Shireen and Joelle, two members of the half circle broke ranks with others in tow, it was Princess Lamia's brothers with their mothers spies, Shireen and Joelle were about to draw their swords, when from behind the market stalls three cloaked women pulled off their cloaks and grabbed Princess Lamia.

It was Delores, Sandra and Savannah, Delores then said "How about you come play with the big girls", then out of nowhere the special guard of light rushed through the gathering crowd surrounding Queen Katarina's spies, the special guard of life was led by Marcus Greene, Xander Blackstone and Jerome,.

Delores then said to Shireen and Joelle "Well howdy, fancy seeing you ladies here, buy anything nice?", as all three females smirked, as all three of Queen Katarina's off-spring were about to be apprehended, suddenly Princess Lamia pulled away from Delores and Sandra, all three siblings swirled around in their capes around, around and around disappearing into thin air, a flash and a bang and all three siblings had escaped, only to leave their capes floating to the ground, only ones that were left of the raiding party was the less able to escape, re-appearing in a haze of a static electricity just before a worm hole, Queen Katarina's off-spring made good their escape through the worm hole that had just formed.

Marcus Greene cwtched his niece and daughter with great delight, smiling at both Shireen and Joelle, Marcus Greene said to both girls "you have done well today, I'm proud of both of you", Xander Blackstone and Jerome looked at everyone as they looked back, Xander Blackstone then said

"A mission well done, not all was achieved but enough to thwart Queen Katarina's plans, time to head back to the palace of light", as the spies were escorted back to the palace of light, Hossagon's were brought forward for everyone, mounting their trusty steeds, feeling emotional and proud of themselves, pulling on their reins started their journey for the Palace of life, on leaving the town everyone smiled and waved to Atmos the keeper of the log, Atmos smiled and waved back, going back to his desk locking the log away, then disappearing to his quarters upstairs, riding back to the Palace of Life, Shireen could feel that this series of adventures were coming to an end, Shireen also knew that this was not goodbye forever but merely au revoir.

Arriving back at the Palace of Life everyone dis-mounted, looking across the grounds of the Palace of life, Shireen seen the keeper of the Beacon of life dressed in his scarlet red robes, disappear into the Beacon of Life, Shireen thought to herself I wonder what things of greatness had been accumulated and stored in the Beacon of Life, as everyone walked towards the entrance of the Palace of life, Shireen stopped and paused then grabbed her uncle's causing him to stop, Shireen then said to Marcus Greene "Have you ever been inside the Beacon of Light?", Marcus Greene looked at Shireen and said "Yes, once, please don't ask any details Shireen as I am able to give any details, it's not because I won't tell you, it's because I can't tell you", Shireen then replied I understand", Marcus Greene replied "Maybe one day you may receive an invite, until then be patient", then smiled at Shireen and put his arm around her, reaching the Palace of Life's entrance, everyone went off to their own quarters to clean and bathe themselves, all the other new Protectors had left for their realms, a medium sized banquet had been arranged for all the Masters of the lower chamber.

Shireen, Joelle and Savannah had been invited as special guests, three balls of explosive static electricity arrived at the Palace of the realm of the Dark Nexus, all three of Queen Katarina's off-spring lay on the floor of the courtyard from exhaustion, Queen Katarina just shook her head in disgust after witnessing the fiasco through her blackbird spies eyes, Queen Katarina did feel some sort unusual form of leniency towards her off-spring, realising that a well organised trap had been sprung and her off-spring had managed to evade capture, that was one blessing,.

The White Witch Queen also watched intently as no one had been injured, knowing the alignment of the three moons of Zerkon was passing, at least for now, a general easing could take place, a certain level of security and awareness still had to be maintained by everyone, The White Witch Queen Nadine sat on her throne contemplating her next move, her next reaction, the decision that she had to make is not one that came easily, interacting with an individual that had no feelings or any sort of compassion for any sort of entities, only a feeling of sheer hatred and evil, Marcus Greene with Jerome followed Xander Blackstone to his study, outside stood two well-armed palace guards, the guards opened up the two heavy large wood doors, once all three men had entered the study the guards closed the doors, Xander Blackstone sat behind his large gleaming polished desk, Marcus Greene and Jerome took their seats in front of Xander Blackstone, Xander Blackstone raised himself up from his seat, then turned to his left, approached a drinks table, placed three gobblets in straight line then poured some drinks, picking up their gobblets, turned, Xander Blackstone walked over to Marcus Greene and Jerome, placed the goblets in their hands, Xander Blackstone returned to the drinks table, picked his drink up from the table then sat down, raising his glass said "To you my friends", Marcus Greene and Jerome returned the same gesture to Xander Backstone, Xander Blackstone started by saying that time was near for us to return to our own world.

As everyone was aware that this was the best tactic not having all Protectors in one place at any one time, everyone knew that the Palace of Life was well protected, though placing one's eggs in one basket was never a good idea, Marcus Greene interrupted Xander Blackstone by saying "Just why the speech we all know what you are saying", Xander Blackstone replied "Patience my dear Marcus ", Jerome laughed and said "You naughty boy Marcus", Xander Blackstone gave both men a stern look of not tolerating any interruption, carrying on with his speech, Xander Blackstone carried on, we as Protectors are going to be called upon a lot more, Queen Katarina is as we speak seeking more and more alliances with other realms of evil , there is a motion before the two chambers for stronger worm hole controls , our wishes will be given to the keeper of the Beacon of life, the keeper will then pass on our thoughts and votes.

If the Beacon of Life agrees the changes will be implemented straight away, bearing in mind that could mean increased activity for all that wear this uniform.

Looking at Marcus Greene, Xander Blackstone carried on with his speech, that means Marcus, that all new Protectors will be placed on the active list.

Jerome said" That's all very well, what about field training?", Xander Blackstone replied "In the current climate the field training will be kept to a minimum, not ideal, until we can recruit more Protectors and increase the Army of Life, then until the numbers are increased, which I hope will be soon, we must all prepared to sacrifice a bit more", Marcus Greene then said "What of our allies?", Xander Blackstone replied that battle plan exercises are being drawn up, generals are making plans, special forces are co-operating with other special forces, there has been no time lost, just kept secret, now is the time for me to inform my most trusted, making it perfectly clear to both Marcus Greene and Jerome that if Queen Katarina succeeds, that no world or realm which included their own would not be safe from her domination and evil retribution, we all know what will happen then.

It was a little while later when everyone in their ceremony uniform met in front of the entrance to the Great Hall, Shireen self-importance rocketed as guards would come to attention every time she passed, the two large wooden doors opened by the Palace guards everyone stood when Xander Blackstone entered the Great Hall followed by Shireen and her uncle Marcus, Jerome, Joelle, Savannah, Sandra and finally Delores, taking their designated seats, Xander Blackstone sat at the head of the table, the formal speeches took place, Princess Joelle was introduced in her Royal capacity as a Princess of the White Witch Kingdom, Shireen was introduced by her uncle, Savannah was introduced by her Aunty Delores, all girls were praised for their acts of bravery, the applause echoed around the Great Hall for all three young women, all three young women bowed in recognition of the honour that had been bestowed upon them by their peers, speeches came from other Protectors of the lower chamber, then the banquet proceed.

Queen Katarina sat while her off-spring were escorted and paraded in front of her, dressed in her usual attire of black battle dress, the Wall of Hate started to shimmer as the anger started to flow from Queen Katarina, clasping her hands she said "I saw what went wrong, I want to know why it went wrong", the Wall of Hate shimmered, then echoed her words, then Queen Katarina looked away from her offspring, walking out onto the balcony that overlooked the courtyard that entertainment her, with the sound of dissatisfaction and hatred in her voice said "I'm far from Happy, however we were entrapped, this is far from over, there will repercussions and revenge", the Wall of Hate echoed her words with the shimmering entity flowing around her offspring, then instructing her off-spring to leave her while she was in a relatively good mood, the shimmering entity flowed towards Queen Katarina, the entity asked" What no punishment?", Queen Katarina replied "It wasn't their fault this time", the entity then said" Revenge", Queen Katarina replied "Oh yes, plenty of revenge, so much revenge that I just can't wait", the entity said" Fun times ahead", the entity glided back into the Wall of Hate then dispersed into a million molecules.

Queen Nadine sat on her throne processing what she had witnessed from the market, she felt that she was left with no alternative but to act, it is not what she wanted or needed. Queen Nadine thought to herself that she needed to make arrangements, calling for her lady in waiting, she reached for a sheet of paper, running her finger across the sheet, as her finger slid across the page words began to appear on the paper, folding the letter then putting it in an envelope, securing the envelope and placing her royal seal, she handed the envelope to her aide.

The banquet finished, everyone made good their goodbyes, Shireen caught her uncle's eye, Marcus Greene walked towards her, he then said "I take it you want to talk", opening a side door, both uncle and niece exited the Great Hall, Shireen then said "Back to reality tomorrow", her uncle replied "Well, is this reality, is the other world we know reality, they are both worlds of reality, you can count on one thing there is never ending evil in both realities, our services will be called upon more than you think, just be ready for the call from the Beacon of Life", Shireen looked at her uncle and said "I can now understand why no rhyme, no reason, is so applicable in these different realms". Leading His niece back inside the Great Hall, Xander Blackstone asked for everyone's attention before their final departure, he closed the evenings event with a small speech, "Fellow masters and protectors, we belong to a unique order, from different realms and worlds, we all know that if the Beacon of Life were to fall then the world and realms that we know would fold, they would be entrapped and ruled by one of Queen Katarina's evil tyrants, this why we choose to serve. I thank you on behalf of the Beacon of Life for choosing to serve, I will remind you that it doesn't matter what, who or how they make a living within the law of the land, every entity deserves fair justice without prejudice, be alert, be ready, you can and will be called at any time you are required to serve", the whole room stood to applaud his speech.

Xander Blackstone then said his goodbye's shaking hands with different individuals, finally reaching Shireen and her uncle he said, "Please come and see me tomorrow, the both of you", both nodded and then everyone left the Great Hall and went to their quarters.

Morning arrived, as the morning parade of the Palace began, it woke Shireen from her slumber, waking-up to an empty bed as Savannah and Delores spent the night in their own quarters, Sandra, she also spent the night in quarters, after preparing herself she opened the bedroom door, all the females that Shireen had come to love and trust, sat having their morning meal, everyone said good morning as Shireen sat down with everyone, Delores said "We had better make tracks in a moment" Delores explained to the girls that a number of Protector's took turns of duty to stay and protect the Beacon of Life with the Army of Life, this was not one of them for the band of family and friends of Shireen Greene, after their morning meal, Shireen and friends made their way out for morning parade, there was only a small parade as most of the new Protectors had already left, there was a blowing of a strange sounding bugle or trumpet or whatever it was, ranks where formed, everyone came to attention, Xander Blackstone followed by Marcus Greene and Jerome followed closely behind with the rest of the Masters, Xander Blackstone then made this speech, "Fellow Masters and Protectors, for those who stay and for those who depart, I wish you a safe journey back to the world or realm you have travelled from and good luck" short and to the point the speech from Xander Blackstone, he then shook hands with all the Masters, this is where the Masters placed their bracelets together and embraced the enthralling journey they had in front of them, a static electrical ball formed around them, as the static electrical intensified and grew stronger there was a sudden flash and they disappeared one by one, Shireen had a sudden bout of sadness, looking around at all who stood around her, not wanting this experience to end, then a voice came from the side of her, Marcus Greene said "This isn't goodbye, just a mere blink of time before we all arrive back here again", smiling at her uncle she said "I certainly hope so", her uncle then said "Embrace every moment of life, even the bad one's as they all have meaning, we that we can learn from", Shireen said " GOODBYE", to all her new found friends, looking around as one by one they disappeared, she felt somewhat emotional as a tear rolled down her cheek,

Marcus Greene placed his hand on her shoulder and said "Time to go, we will just about make it for the barbecue", looking up at her uncle just smiled, before they departed Xander Blackstone and Jerome walked over to Shireen and Marcus, Xander Blackstone said "Marcus, you and Jerome are to call in and see me a bit more often, I miss our little chats" and smirked, turning in Shireen's direction and said " I had my doubts about you, I'm happy I was proven wrong, I dare say our paths will cross again in this world and our world", both Marcus and Shireen smiled in agreeance, he then turned to Princess Joelle and said "Your highness, I believe all arrangements have been made and you are happy with them", looking at her father, Princess Joelle said "Yes Lord Chancellor, I am happy, really happy" smiling at her new found father and cousin, he then said to Jerome and Marcus "Drinks at mine, Wednesday, at around seven thirty pm", both men said "Yes, that would be great", Blackstone then placed his hands together engaged his bracelets, within moments Xander Backstone everyone disappeared apart from Shireen and Marcus Greene, both engaging their bracelets they too had started their journey, as Shireen felt the lifeless feeling she experienced at the beginning of this exceptional experience, a bright light hovered over her head, touching the clear gel like tube that surrounded her, another bright lit up the tube appeared alongside her, there in front of her floated her clone, stretching out her arms and hands causing the tube to change shape, Shireen did exactly the same, with their palms facing upwards they made contact, her clone then smiled as she transmitted every encounter and contact she had made to Shireen, the clone said "I read your sadness, I read your happiness, until the next time, Shireen smiled, the clone then said " Until the next time", Shireen then repeated her words," Until the next time", then the clone disappeared.

Queen Nadine knew that the time was nearing so she made her way to her quarters under guard, walking until she finally reaching her quarters the guard opened up the doors and then closed them behind the queen, entering her bedroom there were two large glowing white doors, placing her hands on the doors she said "Open" in a strong and agitated voice, the doors opened then closed behind her then another set of white doors opened up, everything was white even down to the grass that was underneath her feet, sat on a large wooden bench was a female dressed in a long white summers dress, then these words came from this female "Dear sister, thank you for inviting me to the GARDEN OF SERENITY", the GARDEN OF SERENITY was a place of negotiation, reconciliation, where no magic or weapons could be used without being banished into an eternity of darkness, the female stood up and turned, it was Queen Nadine's sister Katarina, Katarina stood as close as she would dare to her sister, then said" I thought what should I wear for this occasion, then I said to myself virgin white, I just adore virgin white", with an element of rage in her voice Queen Nadine interrupted Katarina and said " What are you playing at, you are willing to murder your own niece for gain of realms and innocent entities just to satisfy your ego", her sister replied with a condescending smile "We all have to make sacrifices now and again my dear sister", Queen Nadine said "I warn you harm as much as one hair on her head, I will track you down and deal with you myself", in her belligerent manner with a smile said "My agenda is my agenda, step in my way dear sister and I will deal with you without mercy", changing her tone and mood in a second , like any good schizophrenic said " Dear sister, why do we argue we could achieve so much together ", turning to her sister Queen Nadine said "Heed my words, you start it, I will finish it ", before Queen Katarina could reply to her sisters stern promise of revenge and annihilation Queen Nadine made good her departure, heading back into her own realm, with the last of the huge double doors closing behind her, thought to herself, the battle is over, the war had just begun.

A ball of static electricity producing a glowing bright white light that filled Queen Katarina's quarters, the blinding light dissipated leaving the Queen back at her palace, the wall of hate came to life, drifting from its lair trying to making a physical entity it best could from alternating molecules said "what news of your meeting my queen ?", Queen Katarina replied "Nothing to concern you, now leave me", swirling around and around the wall of hate then disappeared into the depths of its unknown world.

Queen Katarina laid on her sofa when her pair of black panther guards slinked their way over to her sofa and took their usual position, when there was a loud knock on her quarters heavy wooden doors, Katarina called out "ENTER", her guards opened up the heavy wooden doors, in walked a woman's figure shrouded head and body, walking in a seductive manner that would arouse anyone's sexual drive beyond their wildest dreams, walked towards Katarina, sitting up, raising herself up from her enlarged sofa, standing at a nearby table with an air of regal importance, she smiled as she recognised the face as this female looked directly at her.

Queen Katarina tore the cape that shrouded this female's body, the female was wearing a serving wenches uniform, she then moved in closer running her hands through her hair, placing her hands on her hips then running her tongue down the edge of this females left ear, kissing her gently on the side of her mouth, Katarina let hands wander down over the edge of this females heaving breasts until they reached the hips of this female once more, then said "I've missed you Delores", Delores explained to Queen Katarina that the plan to capture her children had been kept secret and above security clearance and that's why she could not warn her, Katarina accepted her explanation then pushed Delores down on to the table before them, parting her legs so she could move in closer to Delores, Katarina held Delores down on the table while she kissed her neck, looking through a spy with envious jealousy was Katarina's daughter, who had a young girls crush for Delores to ravish her and then return the pleasurable favour.

Katarina lifted her head and could feel her daughter's presence, grinning with pleasure in knowing of her daughter's sexual frustration and burning desire to be with Delores; Katarina moved in on Delores like a hawk about to devour her prey, Katarina's daughter witnessing her mother's cruel display of lust turned away and cried "BITCH".

At the Old Rectory, Xander Blackstone sat behind his desk in his study, dressed casually in comfortable navy blue chino's with matching lamb's wool V-neck jumper and polo shirt, with a cigar in one hand and a whisky glass half filled with a refined malt whisky on the rocks in the other hand, pondering over the recent events, he knew that every person, entity, realm and world had to be prepared and willing to react to every situation that appeared before them, he then stretched back in his chair and carried on enjoying his cigar and whisky.

Marcus Greene putting the finishing touches to his attire, thought to himself how much his life had changed, from being immensely proud of his niece to finding out that he had a daughter, felt somewhat content, fear also set about his body and mind, knowing that endangerment was about to be bestowed on all of them, could only fear for safety and their noticeably young lives.

Shireen and Joelle helped each other to make each other look beautiful, not that took much to achieve, both females admired each other, twirling around so they could make sure everything fitted appropriately, Joelle knew that the secret of new found father and cousin had to remain a secret, just being in the mere vicinity of her new found family made her happy and excited.

Shireen admired Joelle, thinking that she was a brave young woman making such big changes in her life, everyone formulated the plan that Joelle was a new found friend of Shireen, smiling as she looked at Joelle, thinking to herself that she was now a part of something incredibly special, knowing that new adventures could happen at any time, any place, any anywhere, the future and fate of all was to be yet to be defined and answered.

This is where we leave Shireen, family and friends, with the war of words over, plans for defence and war are to be discussed, spies to be entrenched into other realms and worlds, a time of uncertainty was upon everyone involved, only the future will reveal all.

THE END

Printed in Great Britain
by Amazon